PRAISE FOR
LOLA BENKO, TREASURE HUNTER

"An accessible, colorful romp that ends with an alluring hint of another treasure hunt to come."

—*Kirkus Reviews*

ALSO BY BETH MCMULLEN

MRS. SMITH'S SPY SCHOOL FOR GIRLS

#1: MRS. SMITH'S SPY SCHOOL FOR GIRLS

#2: POWER PLAY

#3: DOUBLE CROSS

LOLA BENKO, TREASURE HUNTER

#1: LOLA BENKO, TREASURE HUNTER

LOLA BENKO, TREASURE HUNTER

THE MIDNIGHT MARKET

By Beth McMullen

ALADDIN

NEW YORK LONDON TORONTO SYDNEY NEW DELHI

This book is a work of fiction. Any references to historical events, real people, or real places are used fictitiously. Other names, characters, places, and events are products of the author's imagination, and any resemblance to actual events or places or persons, living or dead, is entirely coincidental.

ALADDIN
An imprint of Simon & Schuster Children's Publishing Division
1230 Avenue of the Americas, New York, New York 10020
First Aladdin hardcover edition August 2021

For information about special discounts for bulk purchases, please contact
Simon & Schuster Special Sales at 1-866-506-1949 or business@simonandschuster.com.
The Simon & Schuster Speakers Bureau can bring authors to your live event. For more information or to book an event contact the Simon & Schuster Speakers Bureau at 1-866-248-3049 or visit our website at www.simonspeakers.com.
Book designed by Laura Lyn DiSiena
The text of this book was set in Chaparral Pro.
Manufactured in the United States of America 0721 FFG
10 9 8 7 6 5 4 3 2 1
Library of Congress Cataloging-in-Publication Data
Names: McMullen, Beth, 1969– author.
Title: The Midnight Market / by Beth McMullen.
Description: First Aladdin hardcover edition. | New York : Aladdin, 2021. |
Series: Lola Benko, treasure hunter ; [2] | Audience: Ages 9 to 13. | Summary:
"Lola Benko seeks out the legendary Helm of Darkness in her second treasure-hunting adventure"— Provided by publisher.
Identifiers: LCCN 2020045195 (print) | LCCN 2020045196 (ebook) |
ISBN 9781534456723 (hardcover) | ISBN 9781534456747 (ebook)
Subjects: CYAC: Adventure and adventurers—Fiction. | Relics—Fiction. |
Supernatural—Fiction. | Camps—Fiction. | Friendship—Fiction.
Classification: LCC PZ7.1.M4644 Mid 2021 (print) | LCC PZ7.1.M4644 (ebook) |
DDC [Fic]—dc23
LC record available at https://lccn.loc.gov/2020045195
LC ebook record available at https://lccn.loc.gov/2020045196

For Emelia Von Ancken—

there are amazing adventures out there waiting for you,

and I can't wait to see what happens.

THREE MONTHS AGO

To: Agents Star and Fish, International Task Force for the Cooperative Protection of Entities with Questionable Provenance, Washington, DC

Subject: Reassignment Notification

We hereby inform you of your reassignment to Siberia. Yes. We know Siberia is very cold this time of year—well, it's cold ALL year—but this is not to be considered punishment. All Task Force treasure hunters eventually draw a hardship posting. We have just accelerated yours. Siberia happens to be an excellent place to think, and perhaps you might want to reflect on whether you made good choices regarding the Pegasus project. But we repeat, this is *not* punishment.

And to be honest, we hope you will not embarrass yourselves and beg to stay where you are. It will not work. Remember, begging is beneath the treasure hunters of the

International Task Force for the Cooperative Protection of Entities with Questionable Provenance. At the very least, we ask for what we want politely and, let me tell you, that is not going to cut it in this disaster . . . we mean, *situation*.

A final bit of advice. Pack warm clothes.
And perhaps extra socks.

Sincerely,

The governing body of the International Task Force for the Cooperative Protection of Entities with Questionable Provenance

CHAPTER 1

BLAME THE FLYING HORSE

IT'S BEEN EXACTLY THREE MONTHS SINCE A mythical flying horse and his stupid bejeweled necklace ruined my life. Yes. You heard that right. Things were going *fine*. We had saved the famous globe-trotting, treasure-hunting archaeologist Lawrence Benko, who is also my dad. Better yet, I no longer had to live out of a suitcase while I followed him around on his crazy adventures. I had my own room, plastered with cute kitten posters, at Great-Aunt Irma's place. I went to an okay school (as far as schools go), but, most importantly, I had *friends*. Real ones! Friends are not easy to make and keep when you're living out of a suitcase. Like I said, everything was *fine*. But in zooms the flying horse, who rudely stomps all over my life, reminding me I am nothing special.

For any of this to make sense, let's backtrack a year to the botched burglary of a valuable statue. I would never have entered the thieving business, except my father was *missing*. Everyone said he was dead, but knowing that was impossible, I was intent on finding him. However, a search and rescue mission required resources I didn't have. Enter the ugly statue of spindly ballerinas worth a *million* bucks, which would have funded my exploits for quite some time . . . until I broke it with my butt falling out a window.

They could have sent me to the slammer for crimes committed against my fellow citizens *and* innocent works of art, but instead the judge decided on a different sort of punishment. I was enrolled at Redwood Academy, a fancy private school in the Presidio. It was to be my second chance (or third or fourth or fifth, but who's counting?) to be a good law-abiding citizen. But Redwood turned out not to be any sort of punishment at all. At Redwood, I met my best friends, Jin and Hannah, and it's a good thing I did because life got *so* much more interesting when they showed up.

Together (kind of by accident, if I'm being honest), we discovered that my father had been kidnapped by an insane person who wanted help finding and using the Stone of Istenanya, a magical rock from an old Hungarian folktale, which was not supposed to exist. But the rock turned out to be *real*. (Believe me, we were surprised too.) And to make matters worse, whoever possessed it had the power of mind control. Not okay, especially when you factor in that insane person I mentioned. We called her "Lipstick," and she was pretending to be a supernice, generous billionaire tech genius named Benedict Tewksbury (actually, she *was* a tech genius and a billionaire, but she was *not* nice). Her goal was to use a chat app she'd invented called EmoJabber, along with the stone, to control the minds of all her chatting minions. Had she succeeded, it would have been a real problem.

But she didn't! We stopped Lipstick, rescued my dad, and retrieved the stone. Yes, you heard that right. We *saved* the world. Sometimes when you are a kid, you feel like things are happening *to* you, without your permission or anyone even asking your opinion. It doesn't matter if you yell or scream or protest—the adults get the only vote. When we were treasure hunting the stone, however, it was the complete opposite. *We* were making things happen.

But then I threw the stone into the San Francisco Bay and everyone got really mad at me, especially Lipstick.

In my defense, that stone was bad news, and humanity doesn't always make good choices. All you have to do is look at history to know that.

In the process of saving the world, I discovered a few things. First, I *like* having friends. It gives me a buzzy feeling inside that is hard to explain. And second, my father works, on occasion, for the International Task Force for the Cooperative Protection of Entities with Questionable Provenance. I know! What a name! Don't even try to say it when you are sleep-deprived. Your tongue will end up in knots. Called the ITFCPEQP for short (not much of an improvement, if you ask me), the Task Force hunts for artifacts that might possess qualities "uncommon on Earth." You know, magical stuff that is not supposed to exist, things that us flawed humans can potentially find and use to make a mess of things. Dad says if you give people unexpected otherworldly power, they go berserk. Us humans like to believe the world is a certain way, and if suddenly that's not true, things get complicated. The Task Force is meant to stop the chaos before it happens.

I'm not inclined to argue with him after seeing what happened when the Stone of Istenanya turned out to be real. But I did argue that he never should have kept his Task Force treasure hunting a secret for, well, let's see, *my entire life*. He apologized all over himself, but only later did I realize he never promised he wouldn't do it again.

Parents. What are you going to do?

So there we were, world-saving, fearless-in-the-face-of-evil rock stars. But what next? Once you get a taste for missing magical mythical potentially dangerous treasure hunting, you cannot go back to the life of an ordinary middle school student for all the doughnuts in the world. And let me be clear, I love doughnuts.

Of course, that was the exact moment Agents Star and Fish, Task Force treasure hunters, swooped in and asked us to come on board as honorary, temporary, supplemental members, specifically to help find *another* treasure.

And that was *just* the opening the flying horse and his fancy jewelry needed to ruin my life.

CHAPTER 2

IT DEPENDS ON YOUR POINT OF VIEW

IT'S DAY SIXTEEN OF SUMMER VACATION. IT WAS supposed to be a summer of treasure hunting and having outrageous amounts of fun. Instead, me, Jin, and Hannah are tucked into the Maker Lab, a tiny studio behind Jin's San Francisco house, created with loving care by his mom, who apparently likes to build robots when she can't sleep. The lab is chock-full of unbelievable stuff for inventing things. And, occasionally, blowing them up. But usually that part is unintentional.

We are the team that won the STEM fair grand prize back in March with an ugly yet powerful electromagnetic pulse device that effectively scrambles anything that requires electricity or a communication signal. But since the Pegasus disaster, we are all wrong. Dad says I should stop calling it a disaster.

"Change your point of view," he keeps saying. "Look at it as a *situation*, a learning opportunity." Maybe, but this is the first time I've seen Hannah since school ended more than *two weeks ago*, so I'm thinking more disaster and less situation.

Hannah is draped across the couch, making spitballs and launching them at Jin, who, in turn, is sucking helium out of a balloon and saying all of Yoda's best lines from *Star Wars*. I dragged everyone here today because we are supposed to come up with new ideas for the regional STEM competition, right around the corner, but instead we are spitballing and Yoda-ing.

And I do mean *dragged*. Before Pegasus, we could not wait to hang out together. We were treasure hunters! We were a team! Now Hannah is obsessed with adrenaline, adventure, and *Bodhi*, and Jin is obsessed with Paul, Paul, and *Paul*. I'm a total afterthought, a discarded toy that used to be fun but now is a drag. When I think about it, it clogs up my throat and I can't swallow right.

"You guys!" I bark from my seat at the wide worktable, tapping my watch face for emphasis. "Time is passing!

Brainstorm! Exciting solutions to our problem of what to make for the competition include . . . GO!"

Jin sucks in some helium. "Can I leave yet?" he asks, sounding a lot like Minnie Mouse. "I have to meet Paul for Minecraft in four minutes." Paul. Ugh.

Aiming her spitball straw at my head, Hannah concurs. "I'm meeting Bodhi at the climbing gym. It's a speed workday. We think we want to free solo El Cap in Yosemite. That would be wild, right?"

Her eyes sparkle in anticipation and my heart sinks. This is not my first attempt to bring us back together, but my friends have *new* friends who are somehow better. Paul is Jin's old best friend who ghosted him when he moved to New York. I mean, he disappeared, vanished, poof, gone without a trace.

But right after we won the STEM competition, Paul reappeared. He sent Jin this woven friendship bracelet embedded with a tiny computer-chip charm, the kind of thing you are forced to make at summer camp, and Jin loves it more than anything, even cake or his little brother. But it's just an ugly bracelet, not an apology or a promise to do better! After the bracelet, Paul started texting Jin as if nothing had happened, as if no time had passed, and everything was exactly as it was, except the geography.

And Jin defends him, like he's been brainwashed. According to Jin, Paul was going through a "transition" when he went radio silent. It was really hard for Paul to move away, and his new private school, Chappaqua Prep or Chadwick or Cheesehead or whatever, was socially tough and he needed time to get his feet on the ground, blah, blah, blah.

But *why* would you take back a friend who has treated you badly, especially when you have better options right in front of you? Unless those options suddenly don't seem so good? Maybe I'm missing something, but I don't think I'd want to be friends again with someone who pretended I was dead.

And don't get me started on the boyfriend, Bodhi! Hannah met him at the climbing gym, where she began hanging out right after the Pegasus disaster . . . I mean, *situation*. She can't go very long without doing something thrilling or she gets cranky, and we were obviously much too boring. I mean, she didn't say that exactly, but we got it.

And we know Bodhi is her boyfriend because she makes sure to remind us at every opportunity. Of course, that would be much more annoying if we *ever* saw her. Which we don't. Bodhi has filled her calendar with an array of thrilling adventures—rock climbing, white-water rafting, scuba diving in Monterey, backpacking the Sierra Nevada—all sorts of thrills I cannot hope to match. Apparently, Bodhi belongs to a family of thrill seekers and adrenaline junkies who have welcomed Hannah with open arms. Or something like that.

Sure, Bodhi is nice enough and hangs on Hannah's every word. And he has an enviable head of curly hair and rich dark eyes and cruises around San Francisco on a long board, which makes him . . . something, I guess. He even took Hannah on a date to the Japanese Tea Garden in Golden Gate Park, and they shared a pot of tea and it was *so* romantic. Barf. But I can't like him because he's completely replaced us. I'm not sure Jin has even noticed, but I sure have.

It's bad. I can't even lure Jin and Hannah to the ice-cream shop, and they both would sell their own mothers up the river for a good cone. I have nothing to offer that compares with Paul or Bodhi. We aren't treasure hunters. We aren't a team. It occurs to me, not for the first time, that we aren't best friends anymore either.

And I blame Pegasus. You know the one I'm talking about, mythical winged horse, Zeus's sidekick, eventually tamed by Athena, the goddess of war. What you might *not* know is that Athena gave Pegasus a necklace. Maybe because Pegasus favored sparkly bling or maybe it was more like a collar with a tag—*If you find this horse, please send him home to Mount Olympus*. But the point is that the necklace is not supposed to exist, and yet, as seems to happen lately with alarming frequency, it *does*.

When the necklace suddenly appeared on the Task Force's radar, Star and Fish were put on the mission. As it turns out, if a human wears the necklace, she can *fly*. The necklace needed to be found fast, before someone ended up as the lead story on the local news and there was pandemonium. People don't react well to the unexpected. Again, I refer you to history.

But finding the necklace wasn't so easy. All of Star and Fish's hot leads went cold. They spun in circles, chasing their tails. And the more they struggled, the more panicky they got. They needed a win. Desperate, they called us. We had found the Stone of Istenanya with only our wits. Imagine what we could do with *actual* resources behind us? They bet on us working our magic twice.

And being honorary, temporary, supplemental members of the Task Force was great! It was everything we imagined. Excellent snacks! Lightning-fast computers! First-class airfare! Not only that, but finding the necklace turned out to be no big deal. Seriously. *That* part was easy.

There is a reason why kids make the best treasure hunters. Adults are stuck in one point of view, and once it solidifies, they cannot see all the gray between the black and white. Changing your point of view is critical if your job is to consider the fantastical.

Jin interrupts my thoughts. "Ow!" He pulls back his hand.

"Huh?"

Jin points down at the circuit I've been carelessly welding, unaware of a long tail of wire coiled right up to where Jin's hands rest on the table. "You electrocuted me!"

"Sorry," I say quickly. "I was thinking."

"About electrocuting me?" Jin blows his floppy bangs out of his eyes.

"Not exactly."

We started our hunt with Jin's idea to dig deep into social media posts about flying people. Yup. And with the computer power we suddenly had at our disposal, it didn't even take very long. Star and Fish lingered around us, offering advice and tips, but mostly we ignored them. Team LJH had this totally under control. We were going to be legends. Bigger than Phoenix and Gryphon, but without the, you know, murder and insanity part.

In less than two weeks, Jin found a boy in Rome who swore he'd seen a man soaring above the Colosseum. For real! Wild, right? Once we made contact with the boy, we grabbed the thread and followed it from lead to lead, post to post, kid to kid, until we uncovered Amira, a woman who sold housewares at a charming outdoor market in Marrakech, Morocco, a small African country across the Strait of Gibraltar from Spain. In addition to pots and pans and plastic storage containers, Amira would sell the occasional magical artifact, a trade she had learned from her father, apparently.

And Amira had the *necklace*. She intended to take it and sell it to the highest bidder because that is how it is done in the magical-object world of commerce. But as soon as she got over the fact that a bunch of middle school kids had figured out her secret, she was willing to make a deal. After all, with the full backing of an enormous global agency, we had *resources*.

We were Morocco-bound within hours, our freshly printed Task Force passports, with the purple cover and the gold lettering, clutched in our hands. Things were happening. We all agreed this was our destiny, what we were meant to do with our lives. It was totally fun.

When we arrived at Amira's market stall as planned,

she claimed she did not have the necklace with her because she expected us the next day. "Come back tomorrow with the payment," Amira told us, "and the necklace is yours." She even offered to throw in some knockoff Adidas sneakers as a gesture of goodwill.

We should have known something was up. We should have seen the signs. We had a deal and now that deal had changed. Sure, it was a minor hiccup, but as Dad would say, the devil is in the details. And we were too full of ourselves to notice.

Hubris is one of those words that sounds like what it means. Excessive pride or self-confidence. In other words, believing there is no *way* you can fail. The necklace practically in our hands, with victory all but assured, we made the mistake of reporting our success to Star and Fish. We told them we *had* the necklace.

Without verifying, which is kind of their fault, Star and Fish turned around and told everyone in the treasure-hunting universe that the necklace was secure. There would be no more trouble from flying mortals. They were so excited by their own brilliance in using us that they even told the big bosses. And the big bosses told the presidents and the prime ministers. The presidents and prime ministers said, "Yay!" and agreed to continue funding the Task Force forever and ever. Mission accomplished.

But it *wasn't*.

When we returned the next morning, with the sun beginning to rise, Amira politely informed us a better offer had materialized and, being as she was a businesswoman, she took that offer. The necklace was *gone*. She didn't even apologize. This shocking new reality came with the distinct sensation that we'd been *had*. And as it turns out, I was right. Lipstick was paying us back for stealing the Stone of Istenanya from her and throwing it into the San Francisco Bay. She wanted us to know how failure felt. And now we did.

Star and Fish had to unravel the whole mess, and at the bottom of the mess was us. As quasi team leader, I tried to take the blame. But Star and Fish were humiliated and angry, and all heads had to roll.

We were immediately dismissed, fired, uninvited, kicked off, left at the curb, abandoned, disowned, disavowed. It was *over*. My friends drifted away to other things, to Paul, to Bodhi. Our team dissolved.

I don't know how long I've been lost in my thoughts, but from the look on Hannah's face, it's too long. And I've probably been mumbling to myself too. Great.

She waves at me. "I *said* we're going. Me and Jin. You can stay if you want. To put Frank 4.0's face back on or whatever."

"You guys are *leaving*?" I bleat pathetically. "But what about regionals? We don't even have an idea."

Jin glances up from texting and shrugs. "Maybe we skip regionals," he says.

"*Skip* the regionals?" I'm aware my voice has gone squeaky and a little desperate.

Jin throws up his hands. "I mean, we don't have a project and we're not really into it. I'm just putting the possibility out there. Don't freak out."

Oh, I'm beyond freaking out. Freaking out is for amateurs. I'm in full-on catastrophic meltdown mode. I clench my teeth so hard I'm surprised they don't shatter.

Hannah, refusing to meet my eyes, mutters something about Bodhi waiting at the gym, collects her stuff, and waves a vague goodbye. Jin, thumbs still flying, leaves for his Minecraft game with Paul. Before they go, neither Jin nor Hannah mentions when we should next get together to work on our STEM project or just to hang out.

And that leaves me alone in Jin's backyard, staring at a mangled Frank 4.0, as if he might hold the answers to my problems. But he has nothing to say, so I shrug on my backpack and head for home. My throat is tight, my eyes threaten to spill tears, and worst of all, I'm out of ideas, a completely foreign experience for me. Maybe it's time to bring this problem to Dad? He claims to be an excellent out-of-the-box thinker, and right now the box I'm in feels bottomless.

CHAPTER 3

THE GREAT GREAT-AUNT IRMA

IT'S A SEVEN-BLOCK WALK FROM JIN'S HOUSE TO Great-Aunt Irma's dusty old Victorian. I came to live here when Dad was secretly tangled up in the Stone of Istenanya mess, and I've never left. Along my route, I meet the usual suspects. Back in my old life, when I traipsed around the world after my father on his expeditions, I never really got to know anyone. There was no routine. There were no familiar faces. But that's all different now. This is *my* neighborhood.

There's Marceau, who owns the upscale furniture store and is always sweeping the sidewalk out front even when there is nothing on it. He throws me a friendly *"Bonjour"* as I pass.

Next is Channa of Channa's Rainbow Yoga, who always waves from her big store window even if she's in downward dog or has her legs wrapped around her neck or something. Tom, or I think that's his name, sits in a vestibule a few doors down from the yoga studio, surrounded by several grungy garbage bags containing his belongings. At first, I'd given Tom a wide berth. He never so much as batted an eye in my direction, but he made me nervous anyway. One day, I spotted a woman in a yellow parka giving Tom a coffee from the place on the corner. In return, he offered her a wide smile. And in that moment, Tom stopped being scary. Now I wave and he waves back.

Dashing around a dog walker dressed in a wool hat, down jacket, and flip-flops, and his seven furry charges, I make my way up the small hill to the half-falling-down Victorian that I now call home.

Home. It never occurred to me how much I wanted one until I had one. Dad felt all kinds of guilty when he realized how much it meant and that it was basically his fault that I had spent most of my life living out of a suitcase. I milked that situation to the tune of a new smartphone because Great-Aunt Irma's cast-offs always came preloaded with tracking apps, as if she didn't *trust* me. Which she didn't. On account of my former vocation as a thief.

Zeus greets me at the door with an accusing "Where's Jin?" Zeus is an African gray parrot with a terrible attitude and a massive crush on Jin. He gets all moony-eyed whenever Jin comes over, leaps right to his shoulder, and immediately begins nibbling his ears and hair. Great-Aunt Irma says it's love. But her voice carries a hint of jealousy because Zeus is her oldest and best friend.

You don't have a lot of friends when you are agoraphobic. That means you don't go outside, and Great-Aunt Irma last left the house sometime during the 1990s, although we can't be sure. She also won't say what it is that drove her inside. According to the internet, which you should never ever consult for medical purposes because everything you search will end up being terminal, even an ingrown toenail, there is usually a precipitating event that drives a person to develop the disorder. Once I asked her what happened and her response was stony silence, very unlike Great-Aunt Irma, and I knew not to push it.

"Where's Jin?" Zeus asks again, fluttering around in my face just to make sure I haven't hidden his object of desire up my nose or something. "Jin! Jin! Jin!" I get why Great-Aunt Irma is a little jealous. Zeus wears his love on his sleeve for all the world to see.

"He's not here," I say, swatting the bird away. "He's busy

with *Paul.*" For my troubles, Zeus swoops in and pecks my cheek. "Ow!"

"Bad Lola! Bad Lola!"

"Who taught you how to say that?" I demand. But Zeus flaps up to his perch in the living room, purposefully sitting with his back to me. Is there anything worse than a lovesick, temperamental parrot? I think not.

"Lola?" Great-Aunt Irma calls out. "Is that you?"

"Yes. It's me."

"Are your friends with you? Or are they with Bodhi and Paul?"

Wait. What? Sometimes Great-Aunt Irma's ability to know things is downright creepy.

"They are with Bodhi and Paul," I mutter, dejected all over again.

"No matter. Come here. Quick!" This is probably a good time to explain that Great-Aunt Irma is not your average great-aunt. Or average *anything*, if we are being honest. Her uniform is shockingly bright dresses and Ugg boots for all seasons. A pouf of white hair sits on her head like a cloud. People say we look alike, but I don't see the resemblance. I never wear Ugg boots. They make my feet sweat.

Great-Aunt Irma spends most of her day coding apps for senior citizens. There are apps to help find your car in the mall parking lot, apps to keep your brain sharp, and dating apps because, in Irma's opinion, why should old people miss out on all the fun? For a person who doesn't socialize at all, ever, she seems to think it's very important that her fellow seniors get out there and mingle. Irma Benko is often called to speak to important gatherings of tech entrepreneurs, but she never goes on account of not leaving the house. Lately, however, she has agreed to the occasional Skype visit, which she reports is a total hoot. I particularly enjoy the stunned looks on the faces of the young Silicon Valley types when they first get a load of her. It's the *best*.

But my favorite thing about Great-Aunt Irma is that she actually *listens* to me, even when I'm griping about math or my stupid Redwood uniform or how Zeus passive-aggressively pooped on my homework. She never tells me that I'm being foolish. She never dismisses my feelings as not being real. And I never get the sense she's thinking about other things when I'm talking to her.

Which is sometimes the case with my dad. Of course, I didn't notice this until I started living with Great-Aunt Irma. And I get that Dad's brain is always chewing on important stuff, but sometimes it would be nice if he focused on me. Is this selfish? Maybe. Right now, Dad is in Peru, in South America, looking for the Florentine Diamond, a 127-carat yellow-green rock that went missing in the early 1900s. In case you are wondering, 127 carats is, well, *a lot* of carats.

The Victorian has seen better days, sagging under the weight of Great-Aunt Irma's odd collection of junk: dusty paperbacks, half-dead potted plants, a life-size cardboard cutout of Indiana Jones, and an extensive collection of ceramic cat figurines and phoenixes—those mythical birds that burn up and rise again from the ashes to start a whole new life. Zeus likes the birds but hates the cats. His favorite sport is to knock the cats to the ground, where they shatter into a million tiny bits. Their numbers are dwindling.

"Lola?" Great-Aunt Irma calls out again. "I said come quick!"

I find my great-aunt in the kitchen, the rickety table cluttered with at least six or seven open laptops. It's about ten degrees hotter in here than the rest of the house. Irma is pacing before the array of machines, rubbing her hands together as if in anticipation of something remarkable about to happen.

"What's the urgency?" I ask.

When she turns to face me, her eyes are bright and

energized. "A lot of old people can't travel, you know? They are stuck at home for health reasons or because they are afraid to go out in the world or they can't find their passports. You know, *obstacles*." She describes these people as if they have nothing in common with her. "So I figured why not harness the power of all these drones that are littering our skies these days, make it so us oldsters can watch something other than the boring garbage on the TV. For example, these military drones see some crazy stuff."

She points to a screen. It's a bird's-eye view of a heavily fortified compound in some unidentified desert. Armed guards stalk the grounds. Big trucks move in and out of a single massive gate. My aunt is offering up a front-row seat to a live-action military intervention against possible drug smugglers or arms dealers or other bad-guy types.

"You hijacked *military* drones?" I ask carefully.

Irma shrugs. "I can also control tanks and other vehicles. But those don't make for great viewing, being at ground level and all. Believe me. My customers will be over the moon."

"Will anyone notice?" I ask.

"Oh, I doubt it. I'm good at what I do." That much is true. I'm living with a white-haired black hat. A septuagenarian *hacker*. Great. This might end with both of us doing time in some remote black-site prison, but if there is one thing I've learned about Great-Aunt Irma, it's that she cannot be talked into or out of much. I will have to keep my fingers crossed she a) doesn't get caught; and b) gets bored very soon and returns to her dating apps, which seem much less hazardous.

The microwave pings and Great-Aunt Irma pulls out a bag of popcorn, ready to settle in and see what sort of havoc the United States Army rains down on this desert compound. She offers me a seat, and while I'd dearly love some of that popcorn, I'm not as keen on the show.

As I leave the kitchen, Great-Aunt Irma yells after me, "Oh, your father called earlier! He has something he wants to talk to you about. Call him back, will you?"

Perfect timing, Dad. I head upstairs to my bedroom to call him back.

Maybe he found a 127-carat diamond?

CHAPTER 4

STAR AND FISH ARE NOT OKAY

To: Agent Fish

From: Agent Star

Level: Priority—Urgent

Subject: Those terrible, terrible kids who are just plain terrible

I can't stop thinking about Pegasus. I know you told me to get over it, but I feel like our good names have been besmirched by those annoying, loud, rude, horrible, terrible, no-good kids. You know the ones I'm talking about, right?

And now we are stuck up here in Siberia. Literally Siberia! I know everyone eventually draws a Task Force hardship assignment, but this stinks of punishment for Pegasus. It's too much of a coincidence. And it was not even our fault! It was those terrible kids! They have gotten us banished literally to Siberia!

Yesterday, I walked out into my new village and almost bumped into a polar bear. A polar bear! In the middle of the street!

I keep thinking of the cautionary tale of Phoenix and Gryphon, those legendary treasure hunters who supposedly found Zeus's lightning bolt, but then Gryphon went insane with power and killed Phoenix, and the bolt was lost forever. Was Pegasus our lightning bolt? Did we aim too high and will now pay the price? More important, are you going to go mad and try to kill me?

Boy, my room is freezing. My mustache is dripping with icicles. Bits of it keep cracking off.

It's all the kids' fault.

So how are you?

To: Agent Star

From: Agent Fish

Level: Priority—Urgent

Subject: Re: Those terrible, terrible kids who are just plain terrible

I know you don't like Siberia, and I will agree that it is a bit on the frosty side, but everyone gets their turn in places that aren't exactly tourist destinations. You are being paranoid thinking we are being singled out. We are up here in the endless frozen tundra doing our duty as others before have done and will do and so on.

And it is nothing like Phoenix and Gryphon! Besides, did that really even happen? Sometimes I think it is just a story made up to terrorize new Task Force agents. The whole "Magic can drive you mad" routine so you exercise caution. And I definitely don't believe the part where Phoenix broke the bolt up into pieces and hid them. Still, it would be great to find Zeus's lightning bolt. Even a piece of it.

That's the ultimate!

And for the record, I have not seen any polar bears, but a Siberian tiger has been terrorizing this small town for ages. I think he is a phantom, a made-up tiger. I think they all spend too much time in the dark up here, and it is warping their brains and making them see imaginary tigers.

Also, sorry about your mustache. Fortunately, as a woman, I don't have to worry too much about frozen facial hair. However, I think my toes have frostbite.

To: Agent Fish

From: Agent Star

Level: Priority—Urgent

Subject: Re: Re: Those terrible, terrible kids who are just plain terrible

I'm having nightmares!

Actually, they are awake-mares. Is that a thing? I see all three of their annoying little faces everywhere. Do you think this is a sign of snow blindness? Or snow insanity? I believe people can go insane if they are kept too long in a climate like this. I would not even know if the sun went out because I have not seen it since arriving in this awful place.

And why are we here to begin with? There are no magical mythical potentially dangerous treasures hidden in the snow! This is definitely punishment. I'm sorry about your toes, but I'm not being paranoid. You are in denial.

Our records were perfect until we got involved with those kids. Flawless! And there was never any mention of Siberia.

The hairs in my nose have frozen and cracked off. It is most disturbing.

To: Agent Star
From: Agent Fish
Level: Priority—Urgent
Subject: Re: Re: Re: Those terrible, terrible kids who are just plain terrible

You need to get a grip! Listen up. We never have to deal with those kids again. The Task Force banned them for life. It doesn't matter that Lola's dad is the famous Lawrence Benko. Even *he* doesn't have enough pull to fix what they broke. This is what happens when you completely screw up.

As for us, we can rebuild our reputations. We need to be patient. To bide our time. To plan for the future and what comes next.

Oh, and I saw that tiger. You might be right that we need to get off the ice.

To: Agent Fish

From: Agent Star

Level: Priority—Urgent

Subject: Re: Re: Re: Re: Those terrible, terrible kids who are just plain terrible

Now you're talking.

Also, was the tiger pretty? I've always liked tigers.

CHAPTER 5

#SAVEOURSUMMER

ZEUS ACCOMPANIES ME TO MY ROOM, A SMALL space on the second floor with a view of the postage-stamp backyard that is mostly weeds. But the room could face an oil refinery and I would still love it because it's *mine*. I love my fluffy comforter decorated with kittens so unbelievably cute I squeal with delight every time I see them. I love my desk, buried in junk—papers, bits of tinkering projects, books, and chewed-up pencils. There is also a pile of random items, like refrigerator magnets and pieces of string, that belong to Zeus. He gets bored when I'm doing my homework and flies around the house gathering things for his ever-growing collection on my desk. It's fine. That parrot needs a mission. Otherwise he sits on my shoulder and criticizes me, and who needs that?

One of my favorite things about having my own room is that I can leave my things lying around and not worry about stuffing it all in a suitcase the moment Dad gets a bee in his bonnet about some new treasure that requires investigation. I love knowing that everything will be exactly the same when I get home from school each day. Except for the items Zeus has rearranged, but that is to be expected.

I lie down on my bed and FaceTime Dad. The screen fills with something terrifying. Oh wait, that's only his gaping mouth, caught mid-yawn. Gross. I can see his fillings. He rubs his eyes and grins.

"Lola," he says.

"Did I wake you up?" I ask. "What time zone are you in anyway?"

"No, no," he says. "I'm only two hours ahead of you down here. If you follow the coast from San Francisco for a very long time, you will eventually hit Lima, in Peru, which is where I am at the moment. It's quite lovely if a bit wet this time of year." One of the great things about Dad is he is an optimist. The glass is not only half-full with him, but it is overflowing, even when the situation he faces is grim.

"I miss you," he says, smiling.

"I miss you, too, Dad." And I do. A lot. But I also didn't want to go with him to South America to chase after some diamond that was probably cut down into a handful of much smaller diamonds and scattered to the winds a hundred years ago. Dad did his best not to look hurt when I told him I preferred to stay with Irma, and he almost pulled it off.

"How is the STEM project coming?" he asks.

"Not so good," I confess. "Jin is with Paul, and Hannah is with Bodhi, and I'm, you know, alone." A third wheel. Superfluous. Unneeded. Unnecessary. Redundant. Surplus.

"Irma says you're moping."

"I am not!" Okay. Maybe a little?

"She also says you've gone boneless and droopy and that you're brooding."

"Chickens brood," I protest. "I am *not* a chicken."

"You know what I mean," Dad clarifies. "Sulky."

"I'm a *tween*, Dad. We sulk. It's our civic duty." Besides, everything is wrong in my life right now. What choice do I have?

"The Pegasus disaster . . . I mean, *situation* happened," Dad says. "Moping won't change that."

I groan. Even he can't convince himself it's a situation, and he's the one who suggested it in the first place! Zeus pecks the screen a few times in my defense. Thank you, bird. At least someone understands.

"But what if my friends have other better friends now and my team is finished and I'm back to being plain, boring Lola?" I blurt.

"Excuse me? You are certainly not any kind of plain or boring. Ditch that idea immediately."

"Fine," I grumble. "But Jin and Hannah and me. It's wrecked. Everything has changed and I don't like it and I don't know what to do."

I am well aware that I'm whining, and I fully expect Dad to take me to task for it. He does not abide complaining, but instead he looks thoughtful.

"Sometimes," he says, "when I'm on an archaeological dig with a team that isn't working so well together, I look for experiences we can share, something to bring us together and remind us why we are there together in the first place."

"I tried that," I mumble. Ice-cream cones, STEM projects, and all.

Dad grins in a way that's completely out of line with how I feel, which is less smiley and more gum on the bottom of a shoe. "Why are you so happy?" I demand.

"I may have just the thing to right your ship."

"A 127-carat diamond?" I ask.

His grin falters briefly. "Sadly, no. But it's still good. They have a summer camp, you know. For future treasure hunters."

A *what*? I push Zeus aside to better see Dad.

"Mean Lola!" Zeus screeches. "Mean! Mean!" He flits to my desk and begins busily rearranging his booty.

"Say that again, Dad. A summer camp for treasure hunters?"

"Well, it's more like a Task Force recruiting-type thing, but it happens in the summer and it's held at what used to be a proper summer camp. They bring people to their training facility on Timber Wolf Island in the Thousand Islands—that's in New York—and try to pick out potential future treasure hunters."

"*How* many islands?" I ask.

He laughs. "It's actually closer to two thousand, but that's a bit awkward to say. One thousand eight hundred and sixty-four, to be exact. It's an archipelago, you know, a group of islands, straddling the Canada–United States border in the Saint Lawrence River, which flows out of Lake Ontario. To count as an island, the piece of land must be at least one square foot and support two living trees. What a hoot!" I recognize what is happening. Dad is off on a tangent. Soon he will be lecturing me on evidence of early homo sapiens found on the islands. I must head this off before it is too late.

"Dad!" I yell. "Future-treasure-hunter camp!"

"Oh. Right. Where was I?"

"The recruiting thingy," I remind him.

"Of course. Timber Wolf Island. Anyway, all the agencies do these types of camps: CIA, NSA, FBI, the Center." There's a pause. Dad shifts uncomfortably on the tiny screen. "Did I say the Center? That doesn't mean anything. Forget it."

My father, a man of many secrets and a really terrible liar. I quickly commit the Center to memory for a future internet search. Maybe they are in the market for kids who can claim on their résumés to have saved the world?

Dad clears his throat. "I think you and your friends are suffering low morale, and I really hate seeing you droopy and boneless and broody. Going to Timber Wolf Island might be just the ticket. Perk you right up."

"Do they even take *kids*?" I ask. My pulse speeds up and my palms grow a little clammy.

"Of course they do!" Dad says with a chuckle. "It's *all* kids. You know how European soccer teams recruit kids when they are not even in double digits yet?" I nod. Sure.

"Well, it's the same with the agencies! If they hear of a promising potential talent, they jump right on it. This is not something they talk about with the public, but it happens nonetheless."

This is so great! But my enthusiasm quickly falters. Star and Fish hate us. They would never let us attend camp. "Um . . . Dad? Although this sounds really fun, I don't think the Task Force would let us in. We are not their favorite people."

Dad waves off my concerns as if they are nothing. "The Task Force *owes* me," he says with a sly smile. "They will do whatever I ask. But Timber Wolf Island will not be easy. It's hard work. Lots of training-type things. And activities. And, well, you get the idea. But if you and your friends want to go, I can arrange it."

This is exactly the sort of thing to get us working together again, as a team, *and* get us back in the good graces of the Task Force. All we have to do is be completely awesome and not mess up at all, even a little. Like, we need to be *perfect*. I let that idea settle for a moment. *Perfect*. What are the chances of that happening? But this is our chance. We cannot blow it.

"Well, what do you think?" asks Dad. "Do you want me to make the call?" Do I want him to make the call? Is he *insane*? Of *course* I do! My friends cannot ditch me if I get us into treasure-hunter summer camp!

"Yes!" I shout.

Zeus does not appreciate my enthusiasm. He glides out of the room, cawing, "Loud Lola! Loud Lola!"

"Fabulous," Dad replies. "It will make everything as right as rain and get your confidence back up. I'll follow up with the parents and of course Irma, but in the meantime take the liberty of telling your friends. I hope they are enthusiastic about the idea. Now, Lola, my darling, I need to get some sleep because I have much to do tomorrow—"

"Wait!" I interrupt. "I didn't even get to ask you about the diamond hunting. How is it going?"

"Two steps forward, one step back," Dad says with a sigh. He looks tired, as if not fully recovered from his kidnapping ordeal. Or maybe the image is grainy. "Although in the case of this particular treasure, it's two steps forward, five hundred miles back. But the scenery down here is lovely." That's just Dad all over, looking for the silver lining in failure. "Now good night, my dear." He clicks off before I can ask any more questions. Not that I would. I'm too distracted by the idea of Camp Timber Wolf! It has to be better than Paul and Bodhi, right?

I text Jin and Hannah immediately. And then I wait.

CHAPTER 6

ALL FOR ONE . . . OR MAYBE NOT?

AND WAIT AND WAIT AND WAIT. NOTHING! CRICKETS! I go to bed and I wake up and still . . . silence. I go so far as to check voicemail for a message, even though making phone calls is *not* done. The initial elation I felt about Camp Timber Wolf being the right thing to bring our team back together basically evaporates like fog in the sunshine. Straddling grumpy and sad, I put off calling Dad and telling him not to bother following up with the camp idea because, like an idiot, I still cling to a sliver of hope that Jin and Hannah will decide we are worth it. For the record, I'm fully aware that slivers of hope can end up breaking a person's heart.

I mope around the house with Zeus trailing behind me, being annoying as only an overly articulate parrot can be. Great-Aunt Irma warns Zeus to be careful, as moody tweens are dangerous creatures. Zeus, undeterred, flutters to my shoulder and pulls my hair.

"Stop that," I grumble. "You're going to give me a bald spot. And I don't need to be friendless *and* bald."

"Lola," he coos, blinking his glossy eyes at me, all innocent-like, before returning to pulling my hair.

"I said stop!" I give him a shove.

He flaps to the top of the bookcase. "Mean Lola! Mean!"

"You were pulling *my* hair!" I shout in my defense. "Not the other way around!" I half expect him to correct me and explain that he does not, in fact, have hair. This is so not my day. I'm about to get really nasty and call him a good-for-nothing birdbrain when the doorbell rings. Zeus goes bananas when the doorbell rings. It does not make any difference who it is. But he is thrilled right down to his pinfeathers to find his dearest love, Jin, on the other side. And beside Jin is Hannah. My heart skips. Maybe all is not lost. Not *yet* anyway.

"Hey," I say casually, rubbing the spot on my head. I don't really know what to say next. I texted them about camp and they didn't answer. What makes it worse is that

I bet they discussed it themselves, leaving me out of the conversation. An awkward silence fills the entryway.

"Come on in, guys!" Great-Aunt Irma yells from the kitchen. "The show is just getting started! I have popcorn."

Oh boy. Great-Aunt Irma is at it again, hijacking drones for her own amusement.

"Popcorn?" Jin asks, sniffing the air. "With butter?"

"Never mind that." I usher them in and up to my room. Popcorn aside, I do not want to have to explain Irma's harmless fun, especially when I suspect it is not exactly harmless.

Jin takes his usual place at my desk, and Hannah flops onto my unmade bed. Zeus clings to Jin's shoulder, chewing gently on a bit of shaggy hair and sighing with delight. Leaning on my cluttered dresser, I shift my weight from foot to foot and focus on the T-shirts hanging out of an open dresser drawer, much too aware of the awkward silence. Hannah finally speaks up.

"It's not that we don't want to go," she says. My heart leaps briefly before crashing as the words sink in. When someone says it's not that they don't want to go, it means they do not want to go. "But it's just that we have other stuff going on right now. Bodhi would be super bummed if I left. We're training for a competition in August."

"And Paul wants to be a team in *Sea of Thieves*, you know, the video game. I have a lot of practicing to do because I'm not very good."

Paul. Bodhi. Me, screaming.

"Besides," Hannah adds. "After Pegasus, I don't know if this is something we are good at, you know? Like, should we even be bothering?"

"The idea kind of makes me sick to my stomach," Jin says. "I think finding the Stone of Istenanya and your dad was just a freak thing. Pegasus proved as much."

Wow. Things are much worse than I expected. How do I talk them out of their doubt when my own constantly bubbles up?

Enough of that, Lola! Get it together. You have to convince them it's worth it. Beg if you must. Whatever it takes!

I take a shaky breath. "Do you guys remember how awesome it was to be on the inside, to be part of the Task Force?" My words hang in the air. There is a beat of silence, during which a memory flashes in my mind. I was looking out an apartment window in a rainy city somewhere in Europe at two girls roughly my age. They were walking to school—uniforms, backpacks, umbrellas—and they were laughing. The girl with long hair said something so funny to the other girl, with red sneakers, that she doubled over in a fit of giggles. And oh, how I *wanted* that, the whole scene. I am not giving up my friends without a fight.

But maybe the wheels are turning and they are remembering? As honorary Task Force treasure hunters, we had resources. We had drivers and computers and smartphones and a big situation room where we could write ideas on the walls in marker without getting in trouble. No one told us to go to bed. No one questioned our right to know things. Or to order pizza at midnight. And the snacks were *outrageous*. Sure, saving the world was good. But also, it was just really excellent.

"It was pretty great," Hannah acknowledges.

"So, do you want to be boring old middle school students or do you want to be *treasure hunters*?" I ask.

"Treasure hunters!" Zeus shrieks, causing Jin to practically jump out of his skin.

"Well, the bird's got it right anyway," I say, rolling my eyes. No one says anything, but I have their attention. I push on.

"I bet there is no one at this camp who has experience like we do," I continue. "We *actually* saved the world. Lipstick was set to turn us all into zombies, but we didn't let that happen."

"That part was fun," Jin agrees, nodding. "Scary at times, but fun."

"Plus, they have a dessert buffet that is open all day long. *And* all night!" That might not technically be true, but, as my father would say, if I'm putting all my eggs in this basket, I better make sure the basket includes a lot of dessert. I grin widely at Jin and Hannah, willing them to forget *Sea of Thieves*, boyfriends, and winged-horse disasters, and say yes to camp. Is it going to work? I hold my breath.

Hannah throws my pillow up in the air like a basketball. "Well, my mother *did* threaten to make me work in the restaurant if I didn't find something college-application worthy to do ASAP." She scrunches up her face. "She said white-water rafting doesn't count."

"Saving the world is definitely worthy," I blurt.

"And *my* parents are forcing us to take an *RV trip*," Jin says with disgust. "Stuck in a tiny tin can with my brother for two weeks. Kill me now."

"Maybe we go to camp?" Hannah asks, glancing at Jin. "You promise it will at least be fun, right?"

"Heaps of fun," I answer quickly.

"I guess we could try?" Jin says.

"What's the worst that can happen?" Hannah asks.

"Oh, I can think of a lot of things," Jin replies. I don't want to go down the road of figuring out all the terrible things that could happen at camp because that will inevitably lead to them saying a big, fat "no."

"You might get a couple of mosquito bites," I say quickly. "But that's it."

"Mosquitoes?" Jin asks, eyeing me. I hold my breath. My heart races. Come on, Jin! "I guess I can live with that. But just a couple, right? Potentially?"

I nod vigorously. My heart races. *Yes!* They are coming to camp!

"Zeus is in too!" the crazy, lovesick parrot screeches.

I point a stern finger at him. "*You* are not invited."

CHAPTER 7

CAMP LIFE, HERE WE COME!

WE HAVE EXACTLY TWENTY-FOUR HOURS BEFORE we leave for Camp Timber Wolf. It took me about five of them to figure out what inventions to stick in my backpack. First in, the handheld version of Frank 4.0. You can never know when it will be necessary to shut down all electronics in the immediate vicinity. There's also a cup-holder umbrella that doesn't seem critical, right up until you dump hot chocolate all over your shoes. There are Ping-Pong-ball smoke bombs and a lavender-infused bandanna with a built-in fan in case you are stuck somewhere stinky and cannot be caught gagging and barfing. I figure at a camp full of teenagers and primitive showers it might come in handy.

And of course, the Window Witch 5.0, a thin, rectangular piece of metal with a trigger-style handle on one end, capable of opening any locked window anywhere. First, slide the metal rectangular piece under the windowsill. Next, pull the trigger and a hook pops out of the opposite end. Use the hook to open the window. In this new version, I made sure the user can manipulate the hook with the trigger, like a video game.

The Window Witch 3.0 was what got me cleanly into Lipstick's mansion on my mission to steal the ballerina statue way back when I was an art thief. When we found Dad and the Stone of Istenanya, I was clear to Dad and Great-Aunt Irma that my criminal days were behind me as I no longer needed to fund a rescue mission. I swore I'd channel my desire to invent, to tinker, into school STEM fair projects and other things that were legal.

But maybe I didn't exactly *quit*. Sometimes at night, when I can't sleep, when my mind is racing too fast over hills and into valleys, I sit at my desk and modify and update and change and improve. I tell myself it's a way to relax, but the truth is, somewhere deep down, I can't say for sure that I won't need these tools again. And when I do, I want them to *work*.

I hoist my full pack onto my shoulder and almost collapse. "You guys," I groan. "This is way heavy already."

"And we haven't even gotten to the 'must have' stuff," Jin points out. Sitting on my bedroom floor, surrounded by piles of gear, we review the required-items packing list. It's long and it might be in Greek, which, unfortunately, none of us know. I'm trying to downplay the extent of the list because I'm afraid of scaring them off. Or at least Jin. As soon as Hannah realized there was the potential for danger, she forgot her doubt. But Jin is a harder case.

"What are hydration salts for?" Jin asks warily. Zeus, perched on Jin's shoulder, eyeballs him adoringly and fluffs his feathers while Jin basically ignores him. Love is complicated.

"Oh," replies Hannah, plucking a packet from the pile of stuff. "These are for when you push your body to the limit and are dehydrated and puking all over everything. Bodhi has them in his climbing backpack."

"Not okay," Jin mutters. "And why fiber supplements?"

Hannah grins. "Because after you are dehydrated and puking and stuff, your body gets massively confused and sometimes you will go days without pooping."

"Days?" Jin swallows hard.

"Or weeks. Who knows?" Hannah shrugs. "Anyway, fiber helps that not happen. Because we might be living on energy bars and granola, now that I think about it. And maybe the occasional orange so we don't get scurvy."

Jin is practically in fetal position. "Scurvy? Like pirates?"

Hannah nods. "If you go too long without vitamin C, your gums turn purple and ooze."

"And your teeth fall out," I add.

"And you get bug-eyed," Hannah says.

"And you bleed under your skin."

"Stop!" Jin yelps.

"Stop! Stop! Stop!" Zeus repeats.

I study the list. "Tree-climbing spikes," I say, holding one up. They are like daggers that attach to boots and allow the wearer to stab her way to the top of a tall tree. "Interesting."

"I hate it when you say that word," Jin whimpers. "'Interesting' means my teeth are going to fall out."

"Tree climbing," Hannah says with glee. "That's more dangerous than rock climbing." As Hannah is our designated team adrenaline junkie, she finds the idea of tree-climbing delightful.

But not so much Jin. He goes a shade pale. "Paul said I should stay home. He said that I'm not the right kid for this."

"Bodhi said I should stay home too," Hannah says. "He said he would die from missing me. I told him that seemed extreme and he better get it together. Anyway, Paul is an idiot." Bodhi might also be an idiot, but I keep that to myself. "And quit worrying. Tree climbing is going to be excellent. We have ropes to dangle from, so you'll be fine."

Jin buries his head in his hands. "Dangling from ropes?" he moans. "I don't know if I can do this."

"Look." I hold up a quick-dry towel and a tube of environmentally friendly soap. "We get towels. And soap." Normal stuff has to be calming, right?

"Which I won't need after I plummet to my death off a dangling rope," Jin replies. Okay. Maybe not calming.

"My father would not let us do this if he thought there was any chance of, you know, ending up dead." I say this with much more confidence than it deserves. Dad is not exactly a conventional parent. He once took me along in a tiny submersible to investigate a sunken ship that was supposed to hold treasures beyond the imagination. (For the record, it did not. The only thing it contained was marine life, happily gurgling around and eating stuff.) Normally, an investigation like this would be done by video, where you, or me in this case, stayed safely aboard a ship watching the whole thing unfold on a bunch of television screens. But no. The ship was not very deep, and Dad wanted to "see it with his own eyes."

"A bird in the hand, Lola," he told me, "is worth two in the bush." Birds? There are no birds under the sea! But he would not be dissuaded. Down we went. And when the tiny submarine sprang a leak, he told me to hold my breath. So while my father would not purposely send us into harm's way, it would be very easy for him to do so by accident.

"There will be other kids at the camp," I say finally. "It can't be that bad. Their reputation would suffer if *everyone* died."

Jin mumbles and grows paler with each item on the camp packing list. On high alert for anything that might derail our decision to go to camp (like fear of death), I decide it's time to go on the offensive. I slap down my list and leap to my feet. "You *guys*," I say.

"Uh-oh," Hannah responds, waggling her eyebrows at Jin. "I sense a lecture coming."

"It's not a lecture," I say. "It's a pep talk."

"That might be worse than scurvy," Jin replies.

I put my hands on my hips. "This is our chance to make them realize they simply cannot live without us."

"They might have to live without us because we might be dead," Jin mutters.

"I will not accept fear from either of you," I say sternly.

Hannah stiffens. "Who said I'm afraid?"

"Well, not you. Mostly Jin."

"Thanks, Lola." Jin glares at me.

As pep talks go, this one is not going to win any awards. I plow forward anyway.

"We need to get psyched. We need to show up there dripping with confidence."

"That sounds gross," Hannah says. "Does confidence smell bad?"

"Just so I have this straight," Jin clarifies. "Fear is unacceptable and I might bleed from my eyeballs and I'll be dripping with . . . something?"

Oh boy. We might be doomed. But out of nowhere, laughter bubbles up inside me like a burp and explodes. Soon Hannah and Jin are cackling like hyenas, and Zeus is buzzing around the room, shrieking.

And for a flash, after such a long time, it feels *almost* like normal.

CHAPTER 8

STAR AND FISH GET SURPRISED

STAR: *Did you get my last text? How did this happen?? I am a good treasure hunter, top of my class, a superstar, the best! I have worked my butt off for this organization, giving them everything. I mean, I have not even complained about being in Siberia! I am that much of a team player!*

FISH: *Are you sure you want to say that part about not complaining? It might be a lie.*

STAR: *You are missing the point! Those annoying kids have been invited to Camp Timber Wolf!*

FISH: *NO*

STAR: *Yes!*

FISH: *But that is where I got my start treasure hunting. It's for special, talented, remarkable, hardworking, diligent people, and those kids are not special, talented, remarkable, hardworking, or diligent. They are just trouble, plain and simple. How did this happen? Getting invited to Camp Timber Wolf is no easy thing, and they were banned for life, last time I checked.*

STAR: *I'm so mad I could spit. Actually, I did spit, but it froze before it hit the ground. Aren't you the one who told me that famous treasure hunter Lawrence Benko no longer had any influence over the International Task Force for the Cooperative Protection of Entities with Questionable Provenance?*

FISH: *I don't think I ever said that.*

STAR: *I'm sure you did.*

FISH: *No.*

STAR: *Yes.*

FISH: *Fine. But remember Lawrence is the best treasure hunter there is and maybe ever was. Well, except for Phoenix and Gryphon, and we know how that ended up.*

STAR: *Don't say the name Phoenix. It gives me chills. Besides, you said that was just a made-up story! As for Lawrence, I never liked that guy. He totally went behind our backs on this.*

FISH: *How would he even find us to ask our thoughts? Does anyone know we're here? Oh, this is turning into a bad day.*

STAR: *Sometimes I want to quit.*

FISH: *And do what?*

STAR: *I have no idea. So while the brats go to camp, buff up their tarnished reputations, and redeem themselves, we sit here patiently and freeze to death? I'm not sure I can do it.*

FISH: *Don't give up. Not yet. Remember, they redeem themselves only if they succeed. And camp is hard. There is a good chance that they fail. A really good chance. In fact, I can almost guarantee it.*

STAR: *Are you saying what I think you're saying?*

FISH: *What do you think I'm saying?*

STAR: *I don't want to say.*

FISH: *Probably you are right, then. We start with Moose.*

STAR: *Will he agree?*

FISH: *He owes me a favor. He'll do what I ask. Plus, he's not overly fond of children, so he might find the experience pleasurable. Running the little brats out of camp and all.*

STAR: *Isn't the whole camp full of little brats?*

FISH: *Yes. But that is not the point. I want him to focus on our little brats. Leave it to me.*

STAR: *I'm going to call you. Where are you?*

FISH: *Ice fishing.*

STAR: *Is that code for something?*

FISH: *No. It's when you dig a hole in the ice, drop a line, and fish.*

STAR: *I have to go.*

CHAPTER 9

MOOSE THE BABYSITTER

THE LOGISTICS OF GETTING TO CAMP TIMBER WOLF are easy. Fly from San Francisco International Airport to New York's John F. Kennedy Airport. Transfer to a smaller plane and make our way to upstate New York. A babysitter will pick us up. The official itinerary used the word "chaperone." What it failed to mention is that plane number two is actually a tin can with wings. Jin almost faints.

"We are getting in that?" he moans. "Does it have parachutes? I think Paul was right. I am not the kid for this." The flight attendant gives him a soothing mantra to repeat while we board the tiny aircraft, something like "The plane flies like an eagle, I fly like an eagle in the plane. The plane flies like an eagle, I fly like an eagle in the plane." After about ten minutes of Jin's muttering, Hannah threatens to toss him out a window to see if he really *can* fly like an eagle. Fortunately, it's a short flight and soon our tin can lands on a bumpy airstrip in the middle of what appears to be an enormous military base.

"Welcome to Fort Big Bang," the pilot says. "The pride of upstate New York. You are now on the twentieth-biggest military base in the United States." If I came in twentieth, I might not brag. But I guess Camp Timber Wolf is on good enough terms with the United States military that they allow access to their airstrip. From a certain perspective, this is scary.

The place is hopping. As we climb down a steep set of stairs to the tarmac, green military trucks whiz by and troops march in formation, chanting and singing. A white van zooms up and practically runs us over. When the driver unfolds from behind the wheel, we get a glimpse of his three-foot-wide shoulders and bulging biceps roughly the same circumference as my waist. His shiny bald head reflects the bright sunlight. I cannot tell his eye color because he wears extra-large black sunglasses, the kind you see on old people after they get cataract surgery. This guy is no Mary Poppins.

"Moose," he grunts, jabbing a thumb into his chest.

Does this mean his name is Moose? If so, we can all agree this is a very apt name. Mountain works too. Or Colossus. He holds out a large hand.

"All electronics." Right. Camp Timber Wolf is strictly electronics-free. This is because they do not want you to be able to call for help.

"Wait!" Jin yelps, pounding out a final text so fast his thumbs might start to smoke. "Let me tell Paul that I'm signing off for a little while so he doesn't worry."

Hannah rolls her eyes. "Bodhi is the one who should worry. With all the tree climbing and stuff, I'm going to come back way faster and stronger and leave him in the dust." For the first time, I feel a twinge of empathy for Bodhi, but I barely have time to consider it before Moose is barking at us. Actually, moose bellow. They don't bark. Whatever, it is loud.

"Devices. Now!" Reluctantly, we turn them over. Jin adds a tablet, muttering something about how I promised this was going to be fun but obviously I lied. Moose asks for a verbal pledge that we do not have additional devices stashed in our gear bags. We swear we do not. Grumbling, so we know he doesn't quite believe us, he tosses our belongings into the van as if they weigh nothing and gestures for us to climb in.

And off we go. Moose is not chatty. In fact, he says nothing. Maybe he's dead? But if I look closely, I can see the subtle rise and fall of his huge shoulders indicating he's still breathing. Plus, we haven't careened off the road, so not dead. A cyborg? That's a real possibility. Jin stares at the back of Moose's giant head as if trying to see into his brain while Hannah lolls in her seat, eyes closed, a tiny bit of drool at the corner of her mouth.

I gaze out the window as the van trundles along a ribbon of road unfurled over the flat landscape and disappearing into a cloudless afternoon. There is not much out here, and by that, I mean, *nothing*. The fields are dotted with cows. We pass a few picturesque farmhouses with wide wraparound porches and purple flowers growing in pots on the steps. The upright silos are abandoned in favor of silage bags, plastic-wrapped livestock feed the shape and size of a silo but lying on the ground. They look like a bunch of Jurassic-era earthworms up and died. But that is it. No cars. No people. No towns. Nothing but stretches of flat farmland.

Jin nudges me. "What do you think Moose will say if I ask for a pee break?"

I squint at our driver. As he is made of concrete, he probably has no sympathy for bodily functions. "No," I reply. "He will definitely say no."

"I should ask anyway." Jin fidgets beside me. "*Should* I ask? I really gotta go. Hey, I have an idea. *You* ask."

Wait a minute. "Me?"

"Yeah. Camp was your idea. Besides, you're good at that sort of thing."

"Asking for bathroom breaks?"

"No. You know what I *mean*."

"I have to go too," Hannah pipes up, even though her eyes are closed and her head is squished uncomfortably against the glass window. "Bad."

Great. But Jin and Hannah are only here because I begged them, so I guess it's my job to take one for the team. "Excuse me?" I begin. "Mr. Moose? We, and I mean all three of us, need to use the bathroom. And kids aren't supposed to hold it for very long because that is unhealthy."

Jin raises his eyebrows at me and I shrug. Maybe Moose is a data-driven person. The mere fact of us having to go to the bathroom might not be good enough. The tires beat out a rhythmic white noise on the narrow road. Nervous sweat gathers at my temples. Did he not hear me? Hannah nudges me with an elbow. *Ask again*, she mouths.

"Mr. Moose?" I say tentatively.

After a pause, "Moose. Just Moose. No 'mister.'"

Six whole syllables! Progress! "Sorry, sir," I reply quickly.

"No 'sir.' No 'mister.' Just *Moose*."

Oh boy, I'm screwing this up and getting on the giant mountain man's nerves and that is not good. And now I have to go to the bathroom too, although it might be anxiety. Hannah's face is doing that weird thing it does right before she cracks up. If she laughs now, we will catch it like a virus and be cackling like a bunch of hyenas in no time, at which point peeing our pants becomes a real possibility. And call it intuition, but I'm guessing Moose won't like being laughed at. He will toss us out of this van on our collective butts, and our dreams of treasure-hunter glory will be over. I clear my throat and sit up straighter.

"Moose," I say. "If you don't mind, we'd appreciate a bathroom stop. When it's convenient for you, of course." He does not acknowledge me at *all*. Doesn't he know the rules of babysitting? You can't pretend the kids you are caring for don't *exist*.

Babysitters. What are you going to do?

I'm about to get mad and do, well, I don't know what I'm going to do, but it turns out it doesn't matter because abruptly Moose steers the big white van onto the sandy shoulder, sending up a cloud of dust. The seat belt strains against my chest.

Jin grunts. Hannah puts her hands out as if she might

fly into the front seat. Moose turns to us, large black sunglasses low on his nose. He nods to the door.

"Go."

We glance at one another. "Go?" Hannah asks. Now, Moose could mean get out of this van forever *or* he could mean go and pee on nature. I'm hoping for the latter. I scramble over Jin and pull open the van door.

"Out!" I bark, pushing him.

"Oh!" Jin says, the light bulb coming on. "He means pee in the *woods*. Sick!" I can't know for sure if Moose rolls his eyes, but I'd bet twenty bucks on it anyway. As Hannah climbs out, she mutters, "Of course, girls are at a distinct disadvantage when it comes to peeing in the woods. Everyone knows that."

And something about her comment lights a fire under our dear monosyllabic mountain of a Moose man. And let me be clear. That is *not* a good thing.

CHAPTER 10

#VANLIFE

MOOSE PIVOTS IN THE FRONT SEAT, WHICH IS NO easy maneuver for a man of his size. And when he takes off his big sunglasses, I know we are in serious trouble. Beside me, Jin swallows repeatedly.

"If you can't handle peeing in the woods," Moose snarls, "you will *not* make it through your first day of camp. The director will send you packing." The moose tattoo along his forearm ripples in a very unsettling way. How is it possible that we've ruined this relationship just by sitting in his van? Does he treat everyone he chauffeurs around in this way?

"We can handle it," Hannah shoots back. "I was only pointing out the inequity of the situation."

Moose holds up a hand to silence her. "Let me think about how much I care about your opinion. Oh right. Not at all."

No one moves a muscle. Moose scans us with dark, intense eyes. Beside me, Jin crosses his legs. Things are critical. "There are rules," Moose says finally, "for being in my van."

Come on, Moose! We're going to do rules *now*?

"Number one: speak only when you are spoken to." Wow. How very 1950s of him—a child should be seen but never heard. "Nod if you understand." Our heads bob up and down in unison.

"Number two: no barfing. Barf can never truly be cleaned from a car. It's ruinous. Game over–level disaster." He wants us to promise not to puke in his car? Okay, I guess. We nod again.

"Third: don't cause trouble. That should be a given, but I've heard about you three from reliable sources. I have your number. I'm watching." Oh *dang*. How did I not see this one coming? His "reliable sources" can only be Star and Fish.

Moose is a minion! His marching orders are probably to get rid of us by whatever means necessary. Talk about high stakes. Getting my friends to camp was important, but in order for us to really get back to what we were, we need to *succeed* at camp. We need to crush it. We need to be inevitable. Moose levels us with a nasty glare. "If you wanted easy, you should have stayed home." Silence descends on the van. You can hear a pin drop.

Or a *parrot squawk*?

"Let me out! Let me out! Let me out!" My stowed gear bag wiggles and rustles. Oh. No.

Moose's thin, sharp eyebrows shoot up in surprise. "What was *that*?"

"Nothing?" I offer. Does Moose growl at me? Possibly.

"Frogs," Jin says quickly.

"Frogs don't *talk*." Moose unclips his seat belt and climbs into the back of the van.

"Out! Out! Out!" the gear bag shouts.

Moose digs in, finds the talking bag, and unzips it. And out leaps Zeus, feathers ruffled, glossy eyes indignant. "Jin!" Our stowaway parrot flaps joyously to Jin's shoulder.

"He *really* likes you," Hannah says flatly.

"What is the meaning of this?" Moose demands. "A *parrot*?"

All eyes settle on me, including Zeus's. "Um . . . he's an emotional support parrot?" I don't explain that it is actually Zeus's emotions that require supporting. "Someone was supposed to tell you."

He knows I'm lying. I can tell by the way he flexes his jaw muscles. Because who carries a parrot around in a bag? But he can't very well chuck the family parrot out the window and call it good, can he? Besides, runaway parrots can have a devastating effect on the local ecology. No matter. Moose looks ready to blow.

"They told me I had to do this for the organization," he mutters, gaze fixed on Zeus. "They told me if I took one for the team, I'd be rewarded later. I'd get to go on the good treasure hunts. I'd get respect. They told me it would be easy. Kids. What's the big deal? Piece of cake. But *nobody* told me there would be parrots."

I raise my hand tentatively. He already hates us. I might as well clarify that we have permission to pee in the woods.

"What do you want?" Moose asks through gritted teeth.

"We still have to go," I say.

"Well, then go already!" he screams. This sends Zeus into a tizzy, screeching and exploding a cloud of feathers into the air. He clings to Jin's shoulder for dear life as we hustle out of the van. If we were somewhere other than the middle of *nowhere*, I might suggest we make a run for it. This whole Camp Timber Wolf thing is starting to seem like a very bad idea.

But I quickly check this line of thought. We *want* this. We *need* this. We can *do* it.

"What did you say?" Hannah asks from a few trees away. "We can do *what*? Not pee on our shoes?"

I swear I did not say that aloud. Maybe it's fatigue, having gotten up in the middle of the night on the opposite coast. And fatigue affects everyone differently. For example, I did not know that it could cause my thoughts to leak out of my mouth without permission.

I clear my throat. "We can do this," I explain. "You know, the whole camp thing."

"Why? Are you having doubts?"

"No," I reply quickly. "All good. Amazing, in fact. Let's go."

Back in the van, I give our new passenger a stern lecture on stowing away in luggage. "Did you even bother to tell Great-Aunt Irma you were leaving?" I ask him. "She's probably worried sick." Zeus does not care. I know this because he turns his back on me and fluffs his feathers in a very condescending way. Great. I can't even text my aunt. She'll probably spread an army of drones across the land searching for him. This could turn into an international incident in the blink of an eye. "Naughty bird," I mutter.

"Naughty *bird*," Zeus mimics. Beside me, Hannah giggles.

I elbow her. "Not funny."

"Kind of funny," she whispers.

We've been under Moose's care for approximately thirty minutes. Everything is going wrong. And now there is a bird.

CHAPTER 11

STAR AND FISH HAVE A FEELING

STAR: *I am speechless.*

FISH: *I really doubt that, as I have never seen it happen before. I don't think you can be. Unless your jaw has frozen shut? I wonder if that could happen.*

STAR: *I thought you said Moose would scare off the kids directly. Fast. Quick. Like, in an instant. Last I heard, they are still there. And we are still stuck in Siberia!*

FISH: *Moose is working on it. Don't underestimate the tenacity of these particular kids. They are not likely to give up easily.*

STAR: *I'm starting to think I should have gone to medical school like I had originally planned.*

FISH: *You'd make a terrible doctor. You don't like blood. Or people.*

STAR: *Minor details!*

FISH: *Be patient. Moose will break their spirits and send them packing. I know he can do it. Moving on to actual business that matters . . . Our Stockholm asset checked in yesterday.*

STAR: *Sven?*

FISH: *Shhh! You are not supposed to identify him on text! That's why I called him the Stockholm asset!*

STAR: *Sorry. My bad. I'm distracted. It's been snowing here for eighteen days straight.*

FISH: *Well, focus. Sven, I mean the asset, said that he heard the Helm of Darkness is in play again.*

FISH: *Hello?*

FISH: *Are you there?*

FISH: *Did you get hit by a car? Drop your phone in the toilet? Get attacked by a yoga goat? Freeze to death?*

STAR: *The Helm is in play and we are stranded up HERE? Are you trying to ruin my life?*

FISH: *No. You do that all by yourself.*

STAR: *Well, then Sven is trying to ruin my life. Why now? And for the record, yoga goats are very relaxing and are not known for attacking humans.*

FISH: *Stop saying Sven's name!*

STAR: *You better tell me what he knows.*

FISH: *It's the word on the street in Stockholm. As you know, after the Helm was stolen three years ago, it disappeared. But it didn't show up at the Midnight Market like we expected it would. And there were no reports of its use. The Task Force back-burnered it as it seemed to be out of play. Gone. Vanished. Lost. Kaput.*

STAR: *Yes. I remember.*

FISH: *But now Sven says it's on the move. He's hearing rumors. There is noise in the network.*

STAR: *You mean the Stockholm asset.*

STAR: *Hello?*

FISH: *The Stockholm asset suspects that the Helm left Sweden on a ship bound for Nova Scotia.*

STAR: *Canada?*

FISH: *Last time I checked.*

STAR: *Can we commandeer the ship?*

FISH: *We could if it hadn't vanished into thin air.*

STAR: *I have a bad feeling about this.*

FISH: *You say that all the time.*

STAR: *But this time I mean it.*

CHAPTER 12

CAMP TIMBER WOLF

WHEN YOUR TRAVEL DESTINATION IS AN ISLAND, boats are required. The white van pulls into the three-space parking lot, identified with a faded sign as Baker's Marina. Calling a rickety dock a marina seems a stretch. But this is northern New York. We have no idea how things work here.

Loosely tied to the dock and bobbing gently in the water is a small blue skiff named the *Raksha*, which I happen to know is the mama wolf in *The Jungle Book*. But before we board the aging vessel, Moose takes each of our bags and dumps the contents out on the dock. A pair of my good socks tumbles into the water and floats away.

"Hey!" I protest, taking a step forward. I really need those! But Moose's glare is enough to send me right back again. Methodically, he digs through our belongings. He shakes the Ping-Pong balls and I hold my breath, hoping they don't accidentally explode in his face. He sniffs the bandanna and makes a face. Who doesn't like *lavender*? Pulling Baby Frank from the pile, he examines it up close.

"It's an electromagnetic pulse disruptor," I explain. "Because, well, you never know when you might need one."

"We made it," Jin offers. Moose looks at Baby Frank, at me, at Jin, and finally back to Baby Frank, after which he hurls my invention into the river.

"You can't do that!" I yell, lunging after it. The only reason I don't fall in is because Hannah grabs the waistband of my shorts.

"Can and did," Moose growls. "No devices. And that was a device." I close my eyes for the rest of the inspection. That seems best.

When I repack my stuff, all that remains of my inventions are the Ping-Pong balls, the bandanna, and the Window Witch. I cannot believe he confiscated my cup-holder umbrella! It is clearly *not* a device! Grumbling, I do as I'm told and climb aboard the boat. The seats are worn, with stuffing peeking through the cracks in the vinyl. In the bottom of the boat, a small amount of water mingles with greasy motor oil, making rainbow-colored swirls. There's the possibility we sink before we make it to our destination. At least Zeus will be able to fly to safety. Maybe he can stage a sea rescue?

The small engine rumbles to life, kicking up a cloud of fumes, and Moose backs the boat away from the dock as we head into the channel. The Saint Lawrence River is wide and dotted with dozens of tiny green islands, as far as the eye can see. The water is crystal clear, and the spray that hits us is a comfortable temperature. Lakes and rivers in California are always freezing, so this is a nice surprise, the first positive thing that I can point to since exiting the teeny plane.

Moose pilots us around other speedboats and the occasional slow-moving barge or freighter as we cruise toward Timber Wolf Island. It's kind of pleasant, actually, riding along on the water. Zeus hates it because it literally ruffles his feathers, but he's persnickety.

As the mainland recedes, there is no way to know for sure if we are still in the United States or have crossed over into Canada. It's a liquid border. There are no checkpoints or passport controls. The boat slows as we approach a large island with a rocky shoreline. A tendril of campfire smoke rises above the dense trees.

"Is this one of those camps where you leave us in the middle of nowhere with an orange and a pencil and we have to navigate our way back to civilization?" Hannah asks. Normally, this sort of question would be tinged with dread, but Hannah's eyes sparkle with excitement. "Because that would be totally *fine*. I love a challenge."

Moose mutters something about how we watch too much reality TV, which is not true because none of us are allowed to watch reality TV on account of it having nothing to do with reality. But I get the feeling Moose does not care about such details.

The boat bumps gently against the dock. There's a sign welcoming us to the island, property of the United States government. Moose directs me to get out and tie up. "A clove hitch," he commands.

"A what now?"

"A clove hitch *knot*," he repeats, exasperated.

"You got it," I reply with confidence as I tie the knot exactly as I would a shoelace. It doesn't look pretty, but it will probably do the trick, provided there isn't a hurricane.

Moose tosses our stuff out onto the dock, growls at my knot, and storms off ahead. The forest that blankets the island reaches right up to the water's edge. The pine-scented air is swarming with gnats, which circle my head enthusiastically. The work of a gnat is very streamlined. Find head, fly around it being annoying. Hey, now that I think about it, gnats have a lot in common with Zeus. I notice there are no gnats buzzing him. Maybe it's a flying-creature-pact kind of thing?

Throwing our heavy packs over our shoulders, we trudge after Moose, passing a series of small log cabins. Nestled into the woods, the cabins, built with faded, rough-hewn planks, appear timeless, like they have been here forever. I expected Camp Timber Wolf to be industrial, smoky, gray, and uninviting, kind of like a coal mine. And while Moose is certainly uninviting, the place itself looks like an antique postcard. There is nothing industrial or smoky about it. A wave of relief washes over me. One less thing to turn off my friends.

"It's kind of *nice*," Jin offers, looking around.

"Super summer-campy," Hannah adds.

"Trees!" Zeus squawks happily. Not only trees, but fire pits and picnic tables and . . . singing somewhere off in the distance? Maybe there is a camp song we will learn while we toast marshmallows and drink hot chocolate? As we go deeper in among the cabins, other campers emerge to have a look at the new additions, like we are zoo animals.

"Um, Lola?" Jin asks, elbowing me sharply between the ribs.

"Yeah," I say. I see what he sees. The campers range from roughly our age to full-fledged teenagers, which is not in and of itself alarming. But these kids look *bionic*. They ripple with muscles and menace. They don't smile or say hello. Traces of dirt on their arms and legs indicate they've been busy wrestling bears or scaling tall trees with their bare hands all day. If success means we have to be better than these kids, I'm a little worried. Okay, a lot worried.

"Hi, everyone," Hannah says, throwing out a friendly wave. They react like she just doused them in acid, recoiling in shock. So maybe no campfire songs and s'mores? I lower my gaze, but Hannah nudges me.

"Head up," she says through gritted teeth. "These clowns are trying to mess with the competition. They probably know we saved the world. And what have they done? Lifted some weights? Who cares? *So* not important."

Hannah's eyes burn with determination. Her words act like a shot of adrenaline. I jut my chin out and smile at the gathered campers. Moose holds open the door to cabin number twelve.

"Stow your gear," he says briskly. "Then you meet the

director." The inside of the cabin is dusty and smells of mothballs. Weak sunlight cuts through the small gaps between the wooden planks. On the tree-stump coffee table is a Camp Timber Wolf binder that might be older than Great-Aunt Irma. Overall, I'd say the vibe is not very welcoming.

After we dump our bags on the floor, we dutifully follow Moose down a dirt path to a larger, boxier cabin. A big CAMP DIRECTOR plaque hangs over the door. As Moose shoulders it open, I make a mental note to ask the camp director to call Great-Aunt Irma and inform her of the stowaway. I hate the idea that she is worried sick about her feathered friend. We follow Moose inside like a row of fuzzy ducklings.

"The new campers, ma'am," Moose says. There is something different about his tone, the slump of his shoulders, as if he, too, is practicing obedience. I glance at my friends. Are they noticing the change in Moose? I can't see the director, as they are completely obscured behind Moose's bulk. I lean a little left, but that does not help. And really, what's my rush?

Because what happens next makes me wish I'd stayed outside. Or better yet, back in San Francisco. Or, possibly, on another planet.

"Fabulous," purrs the director. "I've been waiting for them *all* day."

That *voice*.

I'm not looking at Jin or Hannah, but I feel the shock waves come off them and collide into me with staggering force. This has got to be some sort of cosmic misalignment or a catastrophically awful joke. All we want to do is serve our country and help the Task Force hunt down and capture magical mythical potentially dangerous treasures. Is that so bad?

Moose steps aside, and there she is, in the flesh, grinning like the cat who ate the canary. "I've missed you *terribly*, my fine young friends."

Lipstick.

Tucked in behind the big walnut desk, she has traded her flashy Converse sneakers and rainbow socks for chunky-soled hiking boots and gray wool socks. Her hair is no longer purple and blond and pulled back in a tight bun. Instead, it cascades down her shoulders in blue ombré, similar to the color of the river. But the lipstick is still bright red.

"Tell me I'm hallucinating," Jin says flatly. "That I was deprived of oxygen in that mini plane and my brain is completely screwed up." Zeus screeches like he got stung by a bee and tucks his head under his wing.

"No," I reply. "It's real."

"I did not see this one coming," whispers Hannah, eyes wide. "It certainly changes things."

Remember Lipstick? She is the one who, six months ago, pretending to be Benedict Tewksbury, philanthropist, genius tech tycoon, and inventor of EmoJabber, a chat app that uses only emojis, kidnapped my father in the hopes of using him to find the Stone of Istenanya, one of the magical mythical potentially dangerous treasures that the Task Force is meant to keep out of the hands of regular people. Her intention was to take over the world and turn us all into zombie minion followers. So it's a good thing we stopped her.

But we were under the impression that she was in *jail*! Clearly, we were wrong because here she is, sitting behind the director's desk at Camp Timber Wolf! Whose side is she on anyway? Does Lipstick now *work* for the Task Force? Does that make her an ally, a friend, an enemy, neutral like Switzerland? Am I shouting? Well, I'm surprised, that's all.

I plant my feet and cross my arms against my chest. "What are *you* doing here?" I demand.

"What is that *bird* doing here?" Lipstick shoots back.

"Emotional support bird," I say quickly.

Her face transforms with a wicked grin. "Well, isn't that so *interesting.*"

Oh, I really don't like her. She's as awful as I remember. Jin rests a protective hand on Zeus, who, I think, has fallen asleep. Birds. What are you going to do?

"Aren't you supposed to be in jail?" I demand. "You know, for trying to wreck the world and all that?"

Lipstick waves me off. "Oh, my naive little person. The world is *already* wrecked. Besides, you don't put a person like *me* in jail. What a waste of talent, and talent doesn't grow on trees."

"Actually," Jin pipes up, "they put people like you in jail all the time. You know, criminals." True. They were ready to send me up the river for stealing one lousy, not even very nice statue. Lipstick had much grander plans, and yet here she is. Life is not fair.

"Clueless children," Lipstick says with a sniff. "I struck a deal to stay out of the clink. I'm far too valuable a resource to banish behind bars. I provided the Task Force with details of my operation. They caught some lower-level bad guys and recovered some useless artifacts that they got much too excited about, in my opinion, and everyone was happy." She smirks, as if at an inside joke. "However, part of the deal was to plant me here so they can keep an eye on me and keep me busy. There was some concern that I would cause trouble under house arrest." I guess an island in the middle of nowhere is as safe a place as any to park her?

"And as it turns out," she continues, "I'm good at my job. That's not surprising. I'm *always* good at my jobs. I understand that the best treasure hunters do what they must. And we are turning out potential treasure hunters here who are top-notch. I suspect the CIA will be around to recruit me to run the Farm any day now." The idea of Lipstick at the CIA makes me woozy. How could my dad *not* have mentioned she'd be here? The only explanation is he doesn't know.

"This is nuts," Jin mutters under his breath.

Lipstick jumps to her feet and leans toward us. "Don't you know by now that things are seldom what they seem? The world is full of wonder and terror. *Nothing* should surprise you." She nods toward Moose, who dutifully corrals us out of the office. "You are due on the ropes course in about ten minutes. And you don't want to be late. Penalty points for being late. If you rack up fifty points, you are gone."

Great. They probably dinged us half of that just for the bird. A bead of sweat rolls down my back. Nervous sweat. And we've only been here fifteen minutes.

"Well, it's nice to know the camp director has our best interests at heart," Jin says finally, breaking our bubble of total disbelief.

"The more humiliating our epic fail, the better," I add.

"It certainly raises the stakes," Hannah says thoughtfully. And she's right. It does.

But at what point do the stakes become so high that all hope of overcoming them is lost?

CHAPTER 13

CABIN TWELVE RULES!

CABIN TWELVE IS SMALL, WITH A SHARED LIVING space and two separate bedrooms. Bathrooms are in a central building located about twenty paces into the woods. I do not relish a midnight run to the toilet. Perhaps I can stop taking in fluids at noon?

In our narrow bedroom, Hannah claims the top bunk, which is fine because her nose is literally three inches from the ceiling. She cannot sit up. She can barely roll over. The bottom bunk is a cave, but at least it's not like sleeping in a coffin. Jin's bedroom is a single narrow bed wedged into a sliver of space. By comparison, total luxury.

Tacked to the inside of the door is a laminated piece

of paper, a list of Camp Timber Wolf rules and the number of penalty points campers receive for breaking them. For example, whining will get you six penalty points. Six! And the list does not even clarify what whining *is*! What if you're bleeding? It's as subjective as Olympic figure skating! I don't like this system already. It feels stacked against us. Oh, who am I kidding? Lipstick, our archenemy, *runs* the place. If we make it forty-eight hours, I will be shocked.

Being late for meals, skipping skills sessions, wearing dirty socks—the list goes on. But the worst violation is cell phones. If you are caught trying to communicate with the outside world, fifty penalty points. It's basically game over.

This is what I'm thinking at the exact moment I hear a mysterious *Ping! Ping! Ping!* The blue-bellied river sparrow? The lunch bell? Of course not. Hannah and I turn on Jin, who flushes furiously. He is not good at subterfuge.

"Ping! Ping! Ping!" yelps Zeus, jolted awake from his nap.

"You brought an *extra* cell phone?" I whisper-yell. "It won't even work! And it's an expulsion-level crime!" I jab the list on the door with my finger. "Did you forget that Lipstick is already out to get us?"

"Sorry," he says, nervously spinning his ugly Paul bracelet. "It's only that . . ."

The contraband cell phone pings again. "Shut that thing up!" Hannah barks. "The least you could do is set it to silent mode!"

That does seem to be a fairly major oversight. If you are going to commit a crime, think it through. See the end-game. That's something I learned during my brief stint as a criminal, which is not the same thing as saying I was good at it. But still. This feels like low-hanging fruit.

"I thought I did!" Jin yells back. He's hopping around on one foot like a stork. Zeus finds the ride a bit too bumpy and alights for my shoulder instead. I feel used, but now seems the wrong time for that conversation. What on earth is Jin doing?

Finally, he pulls off his dirty sneaker and tumbles to the ground. Wiggling the heel of the shoe back and forth, he dislodges it and out falls an old smartphone. I am at once horrified and impressed.

"Wait a minute," I say. "That's cool and also, not." Jin holds up the hollowed-out shoe for us to examine.

"It was easy." He's proud, when he should be full of regret and remorse.

Hannah glares at him. "Lipstick and now this . . . this shoe thing?"

"The Smuggle Shoe 1.0," I say.

"Oh, I like that!" Jin exclaims. "Although it implies it can be improved, and I'm not sure how."

"*Everything* can be improved," I respond.

"Can you guys please try to see the big picture?" Hannah asks. "Lipstick is not a member of our fan club. Neither are Star or Fish. Or Moose. They all want to see us fail. And that *phone* is the perfect excuse for them to kick us out."

Jin hangs his head. I can't see his eyes, so I can't tell if he is remorseful or regretful yet. "It's just . . . I *had* to," he whispers.

"Me and Lola can go two weeks without phones." She glances over at me, suddenly suspicious. "Right? I mean, you're not going to pull a phone out of your ponytail or anything, are you?"

I only got my first phone when I came to live with Great-Aunt Irma. It was a hand-me-down, and Irma used it primarily to track my location, which means I rarely took it out of the house, good thief that I was. I can live without one. No big deal. "Of course not," I reply.

Jin raises his eyes, and if I had to label the emotion there, I'd call it conflicted. What is going on? This is not fear of electronic withdrawal. "You should probably tell us what's up," I say. "We're going to figure it out eventually, and this way, we save time."

Jin sighs. It's heartfelt and deep, like he is letting go of a burden. "It's kind of complicated."

Hannah and I take seats on the saggy old couch. "We have six minutes," Hannah says. "Maybe just summarize."

Jin begins pacing the small room, worrying the Paul bracelet. "Okay. Well. I . . . ah . . . didn't want to leave Paul out in the cold, you know? When I told him where I was going and what I was doing, he was so excited about it!"

Hannah snorts in disgust. "He *said* you were destined for failure. Did you forget that part?"

Jumping immediately to Paul's defense, Jin explains, "He was joking! Messing with me, that's all."

"Was he?" Hannah responds, eyes narrowed.

"Go on," I command.

"Well, he asked for all the details, you know, in real time, and I figured . . . well, I guess you can see what I figured."

"I cannot believe this," Hannah growls. "Just because you don't see someone or talk to them every single second of every single day doesn't mean you aren't friends." Wait a minute. Is she talking about us? Was her post-Pegasus rejection all in my head? Because it sure felt real.

Jin abruptly turns on her. "He's my *best* friend." *Is?*

"He pretended you were dead," I say flatly.

"I already explained that," Jin says quickly. "He was *adjusting* to his new life. It was hard."

When I met Jin, he declared that we could never actually be friends because Paul had dumped him and broken his heart. We could work together on a project, stuff like that, but friendship? No way. He was never doing that again. That was fine with me. I knew nothing about having actual friends because I was a nomad and never stayed in one place long enough to make any. Eventually, he came around and I figured it out, and fast-forward to us in a log cabin in the woods. But I do find the sway that Paul holds over Jin a little desperate.

"I cannot believe you put us all at risk for someone lousy," Hannah says with a grimace.

"He's *not* lousy," Jin shoots back.

Uh-oh. The temperature rises in our little cabin. Hannah and Jin might come to blows, and that would be a whole other level of lousy. I hold up my hands. "Come on, you two. This is not helping. But the phone has to go. You get that, right?"

"Yes! Of course! I'll get rid of it. I promise."

Hannah extends her hand. "No. I'll get rid of it. Hand it over."

And this is the exact moment that a horn blasts so

loudly that Zeus vaults straight to the ceiling, all aflutter. In a panic, Jin stuffs the phone between the lumpy couch cushions. “All campers! Ropes course! ASAP!”

Somehow hearing Lipstick’s voice blaring over speakers is worse than even I could have imagined. Dad likes to say that you make your own luck.

But sometimes bad luck happens to you anyway.

CHAPTER 14

THE ROPES COURSE OF DOOM

FOR THE UNINITIATED, A ROPES COURSE IS A SERIES of utility poles and elevated platforms. Between the platforms, obstacles are strung along ropes and cables, like wobbly planks or spinning discs that slip easily from beneath your feet, leaving you dangling in the air. Some courses are high off the ground and require a harness and tether, and some are only a few feet up. This particular one that we now face is almost to the moon, partially hidden in the dense pines.

There are about twenty campers gathered around a table laden with harnesses, tethers, pulleys, and helmets. It's my first up-close look at the other campers, and I'm sorry to say that my initial assessment seems to hold true. They are like minor league superheroes, the kind that get a TV show instead of a movie franchise. There is also a good chance they can do quadratic equations in their sleep, speak multiple languages fluently, are practiced in the art of code breaking, and have read all the classics. Like, *really* read them, as opposed to *saying* they read them.

By comparison, what have we got? As if reading my mind, Hannah nudges me and says, "Don't forget we saved the world."

Moose clears his throat. "As of today, all campers have arrived on the island, so we are ready to begin our full training regimen. You will be tested physically, mentally, and emotionally. The International Task Force for the Cooperative Protection of Entities with Questionable Provenance is uninterested in treasure hunters who cannot take the pressure. If you feel you are one of those people, don't waste our time. Please leave now." He pauses for dramatic effect. No one moves a muscle. "As we train, you will come to know and love the guiding principles of treasure hunters from around the globe. The Task Force was founded in 1857. And while you may think you are smarter than the collective wisdom of those who came before you, you are *not*. You are nothing. Nod if you understand." Heads bob in unison. We are nothing. Got it. "The principles are . . . Expect the unexpected. Understand and respect that which you hunt. Pick your partners wisely. Always have a plan. And finally, most importantly, what we call the Phoenix directive."

Hannah's hand shoots straight up. Moose is so taken aback by the interruption, he accidentally calls on her. "What is Phoenix?" she asks. "Other than a city in Arizona?"

"Huh?" Poor Moose. I almost feel sorry for him, but not quite.

"None of the other principles had *names*," she points out. "I'm trying to be a good treasure hunter and understand the big picture."

There is some muttered agreement among the minor league superheroes. Moose grumbles. "Fine. The cautionary tale of Phoenix and Gryphon, who were the best treasure-hunting team in the history of treasure hunting. There was nothing they couldn't find. All the big ones—the Chrysaor golden sword, the Asi sword, the Kusanagi-no-Tsurugi sword, the Harpe sword, the Ascalon sword . . ."

Hannah's hand darts up. "Anything other than swords? Because that's a lot of mythical swords."

"*I'm* the one telling the story." Moose shoots death rays out of his eyes at Hannah, which she does not notice or does not care about.

"Well?" She places her hands on her hips, waiting. She's going to get us kicked out of here for insubordination if she doesn't be quiet.

"If you'd stop interrupting, I will tell the story. Now, Phoenix and Gryphon also found the cloud-stepping shoes and the seven-league boots."

"Footwear," Hannah mutters. "Big deal."

Moose glares at her. "Not enough for you? How about this? They also found Zeus's *lightning bolt*." A hush falls over us. Even Hannah's mouth hangs open. Zeus's lightning bolt? For real? "But its power drove Gryphon mad, and she attempted to murder Phoenix and steal the bolt. Phoenix escaped with the bolt, but instead of returning to the Task Force as she was meant to, she went rogue and vanished, never to be heard from again. Rumor has it she broke the bolt into pieces to reduce its power and hid those pieces so no one would ever find them."

Moose's eyes sweep over the group to make sure we are paying attention, but he doesn't need to. We are rapt, hanging on his every word.

"Think about it," he continues. "Broken pieces of bolt sitting out there, unprotected. Imagine what would happen if someone got ahold of one? Their power is limitless. The world we know would cease to exist. And Gryphon, who escaped from prison less than a year later, is probably still out there searching for them, driven by a lust for the ultimate prize." Is he trying to scare us? I think he is trying to scare us. I shiver head to toe.

"And so here is the lesson," he continues, "the Phoenix directive. Never go rogue. *Never*. Only bad things will happen if you do." He lets that settle in for a moment. Murmurs, echoing his words, rise from the group. Don't go rogue. It's bad. Got it.

"Now down to business!" Moose shouts, abruptly changing gears. "The ropes course is about team building and keeping your wits in challenging situations. You will be evaluated, as always, so don't lollygag around."

"Lollygag" is the perfect word to crack the tension. A small giggle escapes Jin. Hannah snorts. I elbow Jin and step on Hannah's foot. No laughing. We have a contraband cell phone and a smuggled parrot. We are on very thin ice.

"Your task is to make it around the course twice. I expect you to demonstrate the ability to learn from your mistakes. Like in life, some of you will have to sacrifice your ambitions for the good of the overall team. Team assignments are as follows."

Moose rattles off names. I think they are codenames or call signs, like military pilots or something, because I don't know any regular people named Viper or Galaxy Girl or Unicorn or Hotdog or Bubbles. For the record, he refers to us by our given names, which in this situation somehow serves to make *us* seem silly. We will just have to prove ourselves on the course.

Our group of three is third in line. We are behind high school kids who are not going to win any gold medals for whispering. We hear everything they say despite their best efforts to keep it quiet. There is a girl with a retro Ms. Pac-Man T-shirt and a boy with a slew of colorful woven lanyards dangling from his neck. The other boy has the longest, stretchiest arms I've ever seen, with fingertips that practically brush his kneecaps. His arms undulate like waves.

Jin nudges me and nods toward them. "Do you hear this?" he whispers.

No. Mostly I'm watching Rubber Band Boy and wondering if he ever gets tangled up in his own arms. But now I listen.

"It's *lost*," Ms. Pac-Man says, waggling her eyebrows up and down for emphasis. "Sven—that's the Stockholm asset—said it was on a ship bound for Canada, but then the ship *disappeared*."

"Whoa," replies Rubber Band Boy.

"Rad," adds Lanyards. Okay. I take it back. Maybe they don't all speak three languages and break codes before breakfast.

"Remember, we're being assessed on initiative, quick thinking, flexibility, and all that other stuff. If we are the best, we have a shot at being selected as treasure hunters, for real." Ms. Pac-Man's eyebrows dance around some more, clearly excited. "And there is no way I let any of these ding-dongs get a shot at being treasure hunters before *me* . . . I mean, us."

"What's getting shot at?" Lanyards asks.

Ms. Pac-Man looks set to sock him. "Are you even *paying* attention?"

"I mean, I am, but . . ."

"At treasure-hunter status, you idiot," Rubber Band Boy explains. "So what's the plan? How do we do it? How do we show initiative and that other thing you said?"

"The Helm of Darkness," Ms. Pac-Man says gravely.

"The thingy that makes you invisible?" Lanyards asks.

"It's not a thingy," Ms. Pac-Man says. "It's a helmet. And figuring out where it is will be our ticket onto the Task Force."

"But it disappeared," Lanyards says. "You said so yourself."

"Minor detail," Ms. Pac-Man says with a dismissive wave. "I figure it's on its way to the Midnight Market, where stuff like that gets sold. It's not like you can just plop something mythical or magical on a shelf at Target. Or auction it on eBay."

Rubber Band Boy furrows his brow. "I thought the market was impossible to locate unless you were on the list or whatever. Like, it's always moving."

Ms. Pac-Man glares at him. "And you think I can't find it?"

"Oh, you could totally find it," Lanyards says quickly. Rubber Band Boy nods in agreement.

"Listen. All we have to do is pinpoint the location and tell the director, and they get the Helm and we get to be heroes." Ms. Pac-Man smiles. "Simple."

"But we don't even have the internet!" Lanyards cries. "How are we supposed to gather information with no internet? Is it even possible?"

We are so consumed with eavesdropping that we don't realize they have stopped talking and are blatantly staring at us. "You're the unicorn kids," Ms. Pac-Man says with an unkind grin.

"Major screwup," Rubber Band Boy jeers.

Hannah kicks the dirt. "Not a unicorn," she hisses. "A Pegasus. No horn."

"Whatever," scoffs Ms. Pac-Man.

"It wasn't our fault," I say. "The Pegasus thing." Let there be no misunderstanding—it was definitely our fault.

"That's not what we heard." Ms. Pac-Man erupts with laughter. Rubber Band Boy and Lanyards join in, although Lanyards looks confused by the whole conversation. I'm not sure he's qualified to be here, but no one asked me. Hannah glares at them. I grab her arm. There is nothing to be gained from an altercation over magical horses. Besides, here is Moose, arms crossed and highly aggravated.

"Is this a social hour?" he yells. "Is this free time? Gossip time? Time for chitchat?"

"No sir!" Ms. Pac-Man, Rubber Band Boy, and Lanyards stand at attention, suddenly all business. I think they salute Moose. Jin throws me a look. Are we supposed to do that too? With a flick of the wrist, Moose sends the terrible threesome up onto the course. When his attention turns to us, my mouth goes dry.

"Has the stress of being at Camp Timber Wolf affected your hearing?" he demands. I don't think so because I can hear him loud and clear. They can probably hear him in Canada, too. "I said start on the second course, but you stand here like you're planted." He circles us. I think about great white sharks. "I'm watching you three. I'm watching all the time. Now *come on*!" We race to the start of our obstacle course as if our hair is on fire. Jin's forehead is shiny with sweat.

"Benko!" Moose bellows. "You first. And if you cause me any more trouble . . ."

We do not wait for him to finish that sentence. I charge up the four stories to the starting platform, where I hook myself to a cable and step out on tippy, spinning blocks of wood. Of course, I immediately fall off and find myself dangling upside down from my harness and tether. The ground is very far away. Zeus sits on the platform railing and snickers. Bad bird. I lunge a few times for the tether but can't get my hands on it. Jin laughs at my plight before realizing that it is his and Hannah's responsibility to get me back on my feet.

Jin hooks into the cable, takes a step, and is suddenly upside down beside me. To his credit, he muffles his shriek in the crook of his elbow. Eyes wide, he surveys the situation, noticing, too, that the ground is far away. "Are you okay?" I ask.

"Fine," he replies quickly. "Do you hang around here often?"

"That's the worst joke ever." I grimace. "How do we get back up?" The blood rushes to my head, and I start to feel a little funny. Not funny enough to laugh at Jin's joke but definitely dizzy.

"Well, we for sure don't want to ask Moose for help. Hey, Hannah! Any ideas?"

Hannah balances perfectly on the treacherous blocks of wood above us, as if she is part monkey or mountain goat. "What do you guys think of this Helm stuff? And the Midnight Market? What the heck is that? Like a store for illegal magical objects?"

She wants to have this conversation now? "I don't know anything about a Midnight Market, but I do know what the Helm of Darkness is," Jin says. He swings a little so he can get a better view of Hannah. "It's also called the Cap of Invisibility, but that sounds way lame, doesn't it? Anyway, it's a helmet from Greek mythology that allows the wearer to become invisible. During the battle between the gods and the titans, the cyclopes sided with the gods and made them special weapons to help defeat the titans. The Helm of Darkness was made for Hades, god of the underworld. I'm starting to feel a little nauseous being upside down. Lola, how do you feel?"

"Maybe we table the Helm lecture until we are right side up?" I suggest.

Squatting down on the blocks, which does not seem

humanly possible, a puzzled look on her face, Hannah does nothing to help us. "This Helm sounds serious. Tell me more."

"After the gods won the war," Jin continues, as if this is no big deal, "Hades held on to the Helm. You can't really blame him, right? Anyway, he'd occasionally lend it out to other gods and demigods when they had a need. For example, Perseus borrowed it to hunt Medusa. As he was invisible, her terrible gaze had no impact on him and he returned to the gods with her head in a bag."

"Gross and, Hannah, if you don't help us, I'm going to scream," I say. But she's busy thinking. I can tell from the way her face scrunches up.

"Ms. Pac-Man and friends are obviously gunning to uncover the location of this market place and the missing Helm," she says, almost to herself. "They think if they do, they will get glory, heaps of praise, and possibly an invitation to join the Task Force."

"She doesn't know anything," Jin groans. "They haven't actually figured anything out."

Hannah squints down at us, as if she has forgotten we are here. "Maybe not yet. But what if they do? We need to kick it into high gear and get the intel before anyone else does. She called us ding-dongs. Unacceptable! What do you guys think?"

"I think we'd be in a better position to succeed and whatever," I say through gritted teeth, "if we were, you know, not *dangling upside down*!"

This seems to snap her back to reality. "Right. You guys are totally messing us up. Get back up here already."

"We . . . um . . . can't," Jin explains.

"Well, try *harder*." Is it me or does she sound a little like Moose? That's scary but also motivating. I grab Jin's harness and he grabs mine, and we use each other to get our hands on the ropes and begin the awkward process of hoisting ourselves back up to the unstable and thoroughly evil blocks of wood. Teamwork!

By the time we are upright, I'm drenched in sweat and breathless. Jin glows red with exertion. But Hannah is twitchy with impatience. "Come on," she says. "We have so much work to do. Get *moving*!" She daintily waltzes along the blocks to the far platform, like she was born to do it.

Jin watches her, lips tight. "Why do I feel like everything just got more complicated?"

Oh, it *definitely* has. But the whole point of coming here was to save our team and get reinstated as treasure hunters. And this is definitely a step in the right direction.

Of course, there is always the possibility we make everything much worse.

CHAPTER 15

STAR AND FISH HATCH A PLAN

STAR: *I've been thinking.*

FISH: *Is this a new experience for you?*

STAR: *Wow. You are grumpy.*

FISH: *That is because it is ten degrees in July. Not exactly beach weather.*

STAR: *Well, you are in Siberia, after all.*

FISH: *I KNOW I AM IN SIBERIA.*

STAR: *Okay! Okay! Sorry!*

FISH: *Anyway, while I've been sitting around freezing to death, I've had an idea.*

STAR: *Great! I love ideas!*

FISH: *Yes. I know you do. They are an unusual experience for you.*

STAR: *You are being mean again.*

FISH: *Right. Sorry. Moving on. My idea. The Helm has been giving the Task Force fits for decades. You can't have invisible people running around creating chaos. It's bad for society. But the Helm has been stolen from the Task Force vault twice! It's popular, I guess.*

STAR: *Great idea!*

FISH: *I haven't gotten to the idea yet.*

STAR: *Oh.*

FISH: *Because the Helm is such a pain in the neck, the Task Force would be very grateful to the hunters who find it and bring it in. Very. Grateful. Do you see where I'm going with this?*

STAR: *Yes! Actually, no. Can you explain?*

FISH: *Wow. Okay. I'm proposing that if we go out and successfully hunt the Helm, we will be rewarded for our efforts.*

STAR: *And?*

FISH: *WE GET OUT OF SIBERIA!!!*

STAR: *Oh! I get it now! We could ask for a posting in Maui! Or the Caribbean! Sand! Sun! Surfing!*

FISH: *You surf?*

STAR: *I might.*

FISH: *No. We'd ask for Egypt. That's where the action is.*

STAR: *There is no surfing in Egypt.*

FISH: *There are waves on the Mediterranean Sea.*

STAR: *Big ones?*

FISH: *Can you please focus?*

STAR: *Sorry.*

FISH: *So to be clear. I'm proposing we bust out of here and go after the Helm. If we succeed, there is glory and honor and prestige and reassignment to Egypt. If we fail, well, I don't know what happens then.*

STAR: *Sounds risky. Remember the story about Phoenix and Gryphon and not going rogue?*

FISH: *That was a totally different situation!*

STAR: *How? Phoenix was the best treasure hunter in the history of treasure hunting, and she went rogue and things got bad. And Gryphon was driven insane by Zeus's lightning bolt!*

FISH: *That was a rumor. A tall tale to scare the wits out of the newbies so they toe the line.*

STAR: *Phoenix disappeared FOREVER! No one ever saw her again. That part is NOT a rumor.*

FISH: *I never said treasure hunting was easy.*

STAR: *I do not want to disappear FOREVER.*

FISH: *Are you too chicken?*

STAR: *Do NOT call me chicken.*

FISH: *Are you?*

STAR: *NO! I'm in. What is the plan?*

FISH: *I'm working on it. Stay tuned.*

CHAPTER 16

GOING ROGUE IS A POOR CHOICE

WE DO NOT EXCEL IN THE ROPES COURSE. NOR DO we successfully complete the water challenge. Or the animal-tracking exercises. Overall, I'd give us a D, with credit only for showing up and not drowning. Moose was purposely making our assignments much harder than the other teams'. And the scary part is he seemed to enjoy it. He is clearly on a mission to send us packing. Exhausted, we stagger toward dinner while Zeus gleefully sings Taylor Swift songs until I'm close to strangling him.

"Zeus!" I bark. "Mercy!"

"Tsk-tsk-tsk," he scolds, peering into Jin's ear canals, hopeful to find hidden kale bits or something else delicious hidden in there. Jin gently smooths down a few ruffled feathers, and Zeus sighs with gratitude.

The cafeteria, rustically charming with long bench tables, fluorescent lighting, and the tang of bleach, is buzzing. Just like in middle school, the campers have self-selected into small pockets of people and will end up sitting at the same tables with the same people until camp ends. Everyone whispers and plots over soggy fries and overcooked burgers.

Ms. Pac-Man, Lanyards, and Rubber Band Boy eye us suspiciously as we line up for food.

Other campers stare too, but I attribute that to Zeus, who loves an audience and is puffing out his chest and making a scene.

"Stop it," I warn. "Or I won't visit the salad bar for you." As sassy as Zeus gets, I still can hold a salad bowl easier than he can and he knows it. Jin wipes a small dusting of feathers from his shoulder.

"I bet they are calling me Parrot Boy," he mutters.

"Better than losers," Hannah comments.

"Which is kind of what we are," I point out. I circle around the kids from Cabin Six on my way to the salad bar to fetch Zeus his meal. Their heads are bent over a sheet of paper, and they whisper and gesture frantically.

It looks like a flyer, an announcement for some sort of event.

As I add lettuce and cucumber to the brown plastic bowl, I edge closer. Zeus doesn't eat cheese, but if I lean into the salad bar and pretend to get some feta, I can catch a glimpse of a wrinkled and creased paper that appears to have traveled great distances in a sweaty pocket. The paper's border is sparkly gold, and there is the edge of an embossed silver star.

One of the kids at the table, wearing a Yankees baseball cap, taps the paper with his finger. "*Definitely* a clue to the location of the Midnight Market," he whispers. This gets my attention. "That's their logo. Or crest. Or coat of arms or whatever. Where did you find this? It's, like, *outrageous*. It puts us way ahead of everyone else."

"Confidential sources," another kid replies with a condescending tone.

"You're really not going to tell me?" Yankees asks.

"Nope."

"Dude. *Not* cool." Yankees shoves back from the table and bumps into me. Apparently, I have drifted away from the salad bar.

"Can we help you?" he asks accusingly, as the "not cool" dude slides the flyer out of view.

"Me? No. No way. Just here for the cucumbers."

"They are over there," he says, eyebrow arched. "In the *salad bar.*"

"Right! Of course. My bad!" I smile much too broadly as I head back to our table with Zeus's meal. He immediately flings the feta out of the bowl onto the floor.

"Yuck," he says.

"You are a naughty bird," I reply. He doesn't care. He's up to his bird beak in veggies. "Hey, you guys. I think I saw something."

"Salad dressing?" Jin asks with a smirk.

"No." I explain about the paper that might be a clue to the location of the next Midnight Market.

"This could really help us if we knew more," Hannah says, drumming her fingers on the table. "Do you remember any more details?"

As I rack my brain, something occurs to me. Say we, by some miracle, figure out a clue to the whereabouts of this Midnight Market everyone is suddenly obsessed with. And maybe that clue helps the Task Force secure the Helm. There is no way they let us take credit. There is no way they reward our good work by letting us back on the Task Force. The odds have been stacked against us since Dad got us in here in the first place.

But there is another way.

It's big and I wonder if I should say it aloud because it feels like once I do, I won't be able to take it back. Methodically, I chew my limp fries. Jin eyeballs me.

"She's thinking something," he says to Hannah. "Right? Look at her face."

Hannah peers at me over her water glass. "Yup. Spill it." My pulse kicks up a notch. I should really keep my mouth shut. "If you don't, I'm going to demand Zeus sing Katy Perry next. Really loud."

"Okay!" I throw up my hands. "No singing. But I don't know if it's a good idea. It might be really bad."

"Let us decide that," Jin says, leaning in so his white T-shirt dips in the ketchup.

"Think about it," I explain. "The word is out. Everyone here is trying to figure out the location of the Midnight Market so they can prove their worth. But . . ."

"But?" asks Jin.

"What have we got that they don't?"

Jin stops midchew. "A parrot?"

"I don't think that is what she means," Hannah says. "Go on."

I gesture for a huddle, and our heads come together. "We've got *experience*. We've successfully treasure hunted before. We know how it's done."

"Are you forgetting about Pegasus?" Jin asks.

I scowl at him. "I was *talking* about the Stone of Istenanya." When it was just us and our wits, and there was no outside help, and no one waiting on us to hurry up and succeed, or *anything*.

Hannah takes a big swig of water and wipes her mouth on her sleeve. "I think I know where you are going with this," she says. "But I don't know. I mean, what if it turns out like Pegasus?"

There is that doubt again, the same ugly stuff that kept them from wanting to come to camp in the first place. However, I recognize that the stakes here are *much* higher and the list of rules we will potentially be breaking are *much* longer. "But I could be in. Maybe."

"In what?" Jin demands. "What am I missing? It's like you're speaking in code!"

"Every team is looking for information to help the treasure hunters in the field find the Helm of Darkness," I explain, fully aware that I'm about to pass the point of no return. "But what if we *are* the treasure hunters in the field? What happens if we find and secure the *actual* Helm?"

Jin gasps. "Are you saying . . . ?"

"Yes. We go *rogue*."

I mean, how hard can it be?

CHAPTER 17

SOMETIMES THE UNEXPECTED HAS BIG TEETH

IT DOESN'T TAKE TOO LONG TO CONVINCE HANNAH to go rogue, after highlighting the strong possibility for adventure. But Jin is another matter. He is not fully down with my rationalization that no matter what we do, Star, Fish, Moose, and, most importantly, Lipstick will not let us succeed here. We need to go big. We need to be *undeniable.* Jin reminds us that Phoenix, whoever she was, vanished permanently after going rogue, as in never seen or heard from again. Hannah counters that we didn't care about Phoenix. Finally, we resort to good old-fashioned peer pressure and tell Jin we are doing it, with or without him. Horrified at the idea of being left at Camp Timber Wolf alone with Moose, he caves immediately.

But we cannot go on a treasure hunt if we have no idea where to start. Which is why we need to get a closer look at that document I spied during dinner. And that means we are about to break a lot, possibly *all*, of the Camp Timber Wolf rules by going on a nighttime reconnaissance mission. Oh, and we are bringing our parrot because every good recon mission needs a parrot, right? Besides, if we leave Zeus behind, he will pitch a fit, a loud one, and eventually someone will come to investigate and find us missing. Not good.

"Zeus," I say in my best Great-Aunt Irma voice. "You have to be completely silent. I know this is not your natural state or something you are good at, but everything depends on it." I try to sound grave, but I think I fall short because Zeus rolls his glossy eyes at me. Fine. Time for the big guns. "If you behave, you can have a whole *handful* of kale bits, okay?"

"Kale bits!" he squawks.

"Be quiet," Jin hisses.

"Zeus loves Jin," Zeus coos, snuggling into Jin's neck. Oh boy. We're pretty much doomed.

But maybe not. We've done our homework. First, we

took turns loitering in the window, watching for a night guard or any kind of security only to determine there is none. I guess when you are on an island, the concern that a camper might run away is pretty low. I mean, where would they go? Next, we mapped out a route to Cabin Six that keeps us off the main pathway. Check. And lastly, we did rock-paper-scissors to see who would actually infiltrate the cabin in question and find the flyer. Jin won, so we did it again and the assignment fell to me. Which is good because I have by far the most experience breaking into places where I am not supposed to be. When the clock strikes midnight, we are ready.

It's dark outside, the kind of dark that doesn't happen in San Francisco. A heavy blanket of stars twinkles in the night sky. The looming pine trees look like shadowy giants in the light of a sliver of moon. Water laps the shore in the distance. Somewhere, an owl hoots.

"It's beautiful," Hannah whispers. I nod in agreement, my head tilted up, eyes toward the heavens.

"And it smells good," Jin adds. The air is laced with cedar and a whiff of campfire. I pull my hoodie tighter against the slight nighttime chill.

"Come on," I say. "This way." We creep along the sandy path, single file, giving our eyes time to adjust to the darkness. I keep track of the cabins so we don't accidentally break into the wrong one. When Jin starts mumbling, I'm aggravated that I have to remind him that silence is crucial. "Jin, seriously?"

"What?" he replies. "I didn't say anything."

"You're muttering. Quit it."

"You are hearing things," he shoots back. "I'm as silent as the grave."

"A grave with an undead person in it, maybe," I reply.

"Do you have rocks in your ears or something?" Jin responds.

"You guys." Hannah's voice is about three octaves higher than normal and has a squeaky quality that I have never heard from her before. I might even label it "fear" except Hannah is not afraid of anything, which makes me, in turn, a little afraid. "There's something on the path."

This is not what you want to hear when you are out in the woods at night, in the pitch dark, armed only with a moody parrot.

"What kind of something?" Jin whispers, clutching my wrist so hard I'm sure he's going to draw blood.

Hannah raises a hand and points. There before us, blocking our way, is a huge, dark form. A huge, dark, furry form with eyes, to be more specific. And teeth. Let's not forget the teeth. Big teeth. "Grrrrrr," says the bear.

Suddenly, everything I know about bear encounters disappears from my memory. Was it make a lot of noise? Run? Play dead? Ask the bear politely not to eat you? What on earth is a bear doing on an island anyway? And what's *truly* terrifying is Zeus's absolute silence. I'd figure this is the sort of situation about which he'd have something to say.

"What do we do?" Jin whispers. We don't move a muscle. Behind us, there is a rustling in the low, scratchy blueberry bushes. Very slowly, I turn toward the sound. And there, frolicking to the side of the path, is Baby Bear. She kicks up great plumes of dead pine needles as she spins in a playful circle. Of all the bear warnings, I do remember one, which is never get between a mother and her cub. That our being here is completely accidental will not improve our chances of survival. Bears do not tolerate excuses. Mama Bear steps toward us. Baby Bear frolics.

"What do we *do*?" Jin repeats, this time with urgency.

Besides panic? I have no idea. "Did we learn about bear safety in school?"

"Not exactly." Hannah's voice is still high and squeaky. "If we get gored to death in the next few minutes, I want you guys to know I've had more fun since I met you than in the rest of my life combined."

"We aren't going to get gored," I say quickly.

"You don't know that," Jin responds. He's right. I don't. But I'm hopeful.

"Grrrr," says Mama Bear. Baby Bear snorts with pleasure. She's probably building sandcastles out of pine needles and just having the best old time. We can't stand here forever.

"When I say run," I whisper, "run. Okay?"

"Are you sure that's what we're supposed to do?" asks Jin.

"Yes." No. I haven't a clue, but I have to pick something because doing nothing is not an option. "One. Two. Three. Run!"

Only when we bolt do I realize I should have given more detailed instructions. We scatter in every direction. Jin dodges around Mama Bear and takes off down the path, Zeus clinging to his shoulder for dear life. Hannah dashes into the woods and I make a break for the cabins, hunkering down in the shadows of the closest one and trying to catch my breath. The bears, for their part, lumber away. Now that we are no longer between them, they seem utterly uninterested in us.

But just as my pulse begins to settle down, Jin comes

tearing out of the shadows and nearly gives me a heart attack.

"Are you okay?" I ask, stumbling to stand up.

"No!" he shrieks. "Zeus is gone!"

And we thought Mama and Baby Bear were a problem.

CHAPTER 18

DON'T SEND A HUMAN TO DO A BIRD'S WORK

LIGHTS FLICK ON IN TWO OF THE CABINS. JIN'S yelling has woken our fellow campers, who are ready for anything and anxious to prove it. I bet they'd be tripping over one another for a chance to wrestle that bear. But as fun as that may be to witness, it's time to flee. Hannah intercepts us as we race along in the shadows back toward our cabin. Her shoes squish with each step.

"I fell in the river," she groans.

"Did you see Zeus?" Jin asks, breathless.

"What? No! Where is he?"

"Run faster!" I urge. There are voices. They are gaining on us.

Dodging around clumps of trees, I spin doomsday scenarios about Zeus's fate. He got eaten by the bear. He got lost in the dark. He ditched and flew back to the mainland because the food here is terrible. I am so dead. I might as well have asked the bear to kill me. It's better than what will happen when Great-Aunt Irma finds out about Zeus. Oh, *why* didn't I send him home the minute I realized he'd stowed away? Regret tastes metallic in my mouth. Hindsight is twenty-twenty, as Dad likes to say. Seriously. Not helpful, Dad.

Hannah slams the cabin door behind us and we collapse on the floor, heaving and panting. "Total failure," Jin gasps. You can say that again. But he won't because the first time was hard enough.

I stagger to my feet. "Brainstorm," I say. "Solutions to this problem include . . ." I wait for my friends to throw out ideas about how we might find Zeus, but all I hear is their ragged breathing. A cold spasm of fear makes me shiver. Zeus is a pain, but the idea of him out in this big, dark, bear-infested forest all by himself makes me queasy. He's a house pet. He has no skills other than a sharp tongue. He's going to get eaten by an owl! I flop down beside Hannah and bury my head in my hands.

Think, Lola, think!

Outside, a branch brushes against the cabin window, tapping out an eerie Morse code. This is all my fault. If I hadn't insisted on going rogue, Zeus would not have become a bear appetizer.

Tap—tap—tap. Tap—tap—tap. "Will someone stop that branch before it drives me insane?" I shout. Hannah glances at Jin, eyebrows raised, as Jin slowly rises from the ground to deal with the window. But when he throws it open, a tangle of color and noise rushes in. Jin yelps in surprise and Hannah ducks. My first thought is that the bear is back to shred us to ribbons. I throw my arms in front of my face to ward off whatever just plowed through our window.

"Lola! Lola! Lola!"

Zeus? In a flurry of feathers, the mighty Zeus alights on my shoulder. A folded piece of paper dangles from his beak. Jin rushes over and hugs us both, but let's be honest, this overt display of affection is really for the bird. Gently, I pull the paper from Zeus's sharp beak. Even before I unfold it, I *know* what it is. But how this birdbrained bird knew how and where and what is utterly beyond me. Zeus gives me a smug, condescending look. Don't send a human to do a bird's work. Okay. I deserve it.

"Did he *really*?" Hannah asks, standing over my shoulder, looking at the flyer.

"He did," I confirm. "Don't ask how."

"I won't," she says.

I stroke Zeus's head. "Good bird," I say softly.

"Lola," he coos, and takes a quick nip of my ear. Ouch! Talk about a complicated relationship.

"Is it the same paper you saw in the cafeteria?" Jin asks. Up close, it is colorful like a peacock, a spray of embossed, rainbow-colored stars twinkling as if somehow lit from within. In the center is a bloodred circle, in a braided pattern, enclosing the letters *MM*, done in swirling emerald-green calligraphy.

"Yes," I reply.

Jin shakes his head. "That's some bird," he says, voice full of awe. If we keep this up, Zeus is going to get a big head and become even more intolerable than he is now. We gather around the small tree-stump coffee table and smooth out the wrinkled flyer.

We study it intently until finally Jin says, "So it doesn't actually have any information on it."

He's right. I half expected a time, address, and RSVP request for the Midnight Market. But that would have been too easy. "I think we should go to bed," Hannah says with a defeated sigh. "This is pointless and I'm tired."

Outside, the crickets chirp maniacally. I'm about to

agree with Hannah's assessment when something occurs to me. Dad loves a good cave drawing or hieroglyphics. He has lectured me a thousand times on how rudimentary pictures were used to tell a story or give directions or level a warning. Of course, when I told him that's what *emojis* are for too, his head nearly exploded.

"Not the same!" he thundered. But whatever, that is not the point. The point *is*, what if the information on the page *does* actually tell us where the market is?

Hannah digs an elbow into my ribs. "You're muttering."

I am? Embarrassing. "Okay. How about if this is all the information we need, but we don't understand it?"

"Like, the market is out in the stars?" Jin asks. "You can't Uber a rocket ship, you know."

"That's not it," I reply. "The stars *mean* something and we have to figure out what. Like, a clue or a cipher or a puzzle."

"Oh," he says, like a light bulb went on. "Duh. I get it."

"But what?" asks Hannah. Well, honestly, I have no idea. The possible meaning of a bunch of rainbow stars seems endless. I deflate.

"I would *kill* for the internet right now," Hannah complains. "It's like we are stuck in the 1980s or something awful like that."

"We could use the phone," Jin says after a pause.

We debate the prohibited use of the internet well into the wee hours of the night. Oh, who am I kidding? We do nothing of the sort, pouncing right on that phone without pausing to consider the consequences for even a second.

Our trespasses are adding up. Sneaking around at night. Stealing the flyer. Scaring the bears. Using the internet. Dad likes to say that eventually you pay the piper, which means that at some point there will be consequences for our actions. But being as we intend to go rogue, our mountain of misdeeds seems inconsequential.

We are in "all or nothing" territory now.

CHAPTER 19

A SLIPPERY SLOPE. DOWN WHICH WE CAREEN. OUT OF CONTROL.

AS WE HUDDLE AROUND THE TINY BLUE SCREEN, searching for what the flyer might mean, I feel that familiar buzz, the sense that we are onto something, all pulling in the same direction, combining our energy and smarts to create something larger than ourselves. We are ready to do what must be done. We will uncover what these stars mean, no matter *what*.

Or we won't. Forty-five minutes later, Jin is snoring on the couch, muttering about Paul, with a fast-asleep Zeus tucked into his armpit. And I keep pinching myself to stay awake.

"I get that technology is not the answer to all our

problems," Hannah says, rubbing her eyes. "But I really thought it might be in this case."

"Keep searching," I chide. "This star pattern means *something.*"

While she searches, I study the flyer, looking for an embedded code or a secret message written in the stars. So far, zippo. Suddenly, Hannah exhales sharply. I perk up. But her shoulders sag just as quickly. "I thought I had something," she says. "A constellation that is no longer a constellation."

"Wait. You can get fired from being a constellation?" Is there really no such thing as job security these days?

"It's kind of like Pluto," she explains. "It used to be a planet, but then it got voted off the island. Pluto itself hasn't changed, but how we think about it has. It doesn't matter. Our stars don't quite match anyway."

Back to square one. A half hour later, Hannah leans over and bangs her forehead gently on the coffee table. Uh-oh. "We've checked every constellation," she grumbles, "every weird space anomaly, every black hole and known galaxy and star map. I feel like a time traveler, I've been across the universe so many times. And for what? *Nothing.* I'm so tired I can't even yawn."

But she doesn't chuck the phone across the room and

collapse in a heap. Instead, she resumes scrolling through endless star images in hopes of stumbling upon something that corresponds to the images on the paper. I'm exhausted too but also afraid to give up. It's like the end of a string is floating inches beyond my grasp and if I could grab hold and pull, this mystery would unravel before us.

"Maybe it's really just a pretty picture with stars," Hannah says dejectedly. "I want to go to bed. My thumbs hurt from scrolling. And my eyes hurt. And my feet are wet."

"You fell in the river."

"Don't remind me."

"Do you want to go to bed?" I ask quietly.

"No way," Hannah says. "We are in this now. Let's keep looking."

But at some point our efforts become hopeless. Hannah slumps over Jin, dead asleep. My vision swims in and out of focus, which is why I dismiss the ghostly image of Lipstick at our cabin window. Obviously, I'm hallucinating. It's like those dreams I sometimes have where she is lurking in the shadows ready to kidnap me. I always try to scream, but my voice is gone. This is the point where I usually wake up, sweaty, heart pounding. That Lipstick thrives in my head is more than a little disturbing.

I rub my eyes to make her go away. Nope. She's still

there. Now she's smiling and beckoning me. What the heck? I shake my head vigorously. But she remains at the window, no longer smiling, and gesturing a bit more aggressively.

Oh no. Is she *real*? Like in the dreams, I break out in an instant sweat, and my heart thunders in my ears. I leave my friends and bird snoozing on the couch and tiptoe to the cabin door. If it turns out she actually is a hallucination, I really don't want them to know I'm seeing things.

The door creaks loudly on its rusty hinges as I pull it open. Cringing, I throw a glance over my shoulder, sure Zeus is going to wake up and start bellowing. But everyone remains still and peaceful. I peer out into the darkness. The day's humidity still clings to the air. I glance left. Nothing. I glance right. Nothing. My heart slows. Lipstick is all in my head. It's fine. All good.

Except it's not. Suddenly, a hand clamps over my mouth and I'm dragged out of the cabin. The door slams shut behind me. I try to scream, but nothing comes out. When people talk about dreams coming true, I'm pretty sure this is not what they mean.

"You're spitting all over my hand," Lipstick says. "It's disgusting."

Wait a minute. She pulls me from my cabin in the dead

of night and *then* tries to make me feel bad? That is not okay. "Let me go," I mumble through her fingers.

"No screaming. Promise."

"I promise." She still does not let go. Is she waiting for a blood oath or something? "I *swear*."

Finally, she releases me. I shake myself out like a dog with fleas. Lipstick watches curiously. "Are you having a seizure?" she asks.

I refuse to answer that. "What are you doing here? It's the middle of the night."

"I know," she says, giving me a sly grin. "I also know you took an evening stroll around campus. You met Daisy and Pipsqueak? They swim over from the mainland for the berries. Quite unusual."

The bears have *names*? They *swim* here? I struggle to come up with an appropriate response, but I'm busy berating myself for being so stupid. Why did we think for even a *second* that something could happen at Camp Timber Wolf without Lipstick knowing about it?

"Pipsqueak?" I gulp after a long pause. "Really?"

"The part with the bird was a neat trick," she says. "I'm curious how you trained him to fetch. All the parrots I've ever known have too much dignity for parlor tricks."

Well, Zeus has no dignity, let's start with that. As for

his fetching skills, it's a mystery to me, too. But I don't want to look clueless. Lipstick already has the upper hand. Actually, she has *all* the hands. So I shrug like a fetching parrot is no big deal.

"Well, never mind that." She waves off the parrot. "Let's move on to the faintly blue glow emanating from your cabin. Couldn't survive forty-eight hours without an infusion of YouTube videos? Or social media with your BFFs? Or maybe the latest episode of whatever garbage you youngsters are streaming these days? Or was it something else entirely? Something *much* more interesting."

This is it, the part where she kicks us out of Camp Timber Wolf. And we totally deserve it. What is *wrong* with us? Why did I think going rogue would solve our problems? My heart sinks, my dreams of chasing down magical mythical potentially dangerous treasures evaporating like fog in sunshine. We screwed up and got caught. It's like when I was trying to be a thief. Screw up. Get caught. My chin drops to my chest. I feel about two inches tall.

"Oh, cut the drama," Lipstick says with disgust. "It's beneath you." I wish she'd get to the expulsion part. Standing here waiting for the axe to fall is exhausting. Plus, my thin hoodie is no match for the damp night air. I shift my weight from foot to foot. What am I going to tell Jin and

Hannah when they wake up? Our team is just starting to get back in the groove and now *this*.

I think I might cry, but no way Lipstick tolerates blubbering. I bite my lip to keep the tears at bay. But she doesn't kick us out, at least not yet.

"I've been thinking," she says. "Well, I'm *always* thinking, and usually it's brilliant things, but that's a given, right?" I nod because it's not like I'm going to disagree with her. "I need something done, and unfortunately, you might be the only kids who can do it." She makes a face like the words taste bad.

"Naturally, you've heard buzz about the Helm of Darkness?" she continues. "The whole camp is *seething* with it." Her eyes twinkle as if Camp Timber Wolf in upheaval is such good fun.

I cock my head to the left. "Yeah."

"As you probably know, the acquisition of magical objects is very competitive," Lipstick says. "And while I'm currently sidelined"—she gestures at her ankle monitor—"I still hate losing, especially to *certain* people." Her eyes darken and her hands ball into tight fists. "I do not want this *certain* person, a particularly annoying competitor, to acquire the Helm. If she does, she will gloat and hold it over me forever, an absolutely intolerable situation. What

I want is for her to *fail*." She pauses. The orchestra of night-time crickets plays on. I don't move a muscle. "That's what I want. Now, Lola Benko, tell me what *you* want?"

What? Aren't we talking about her nemesis, whoever that unfortunate soul is, getting the Helm while Lipstick is trapped on an island, under house arrest and surrounded by a bunch of overmuscled kids? No? She waits quietly, and I get the feeling I'm actually supposed to answer.

Okay, then. What do I *want*? It's kind of a broad question. I mean, right now I want a warmer hoodie and socks. I also don't want to worry that my friends are going to ditch me. And I want my father to be safe. And I want Great-Aunt Irma to not kill me over the Zeus thing and also to be brave enough to go outside. And I'd like some chocolate ice cream.

But I don't think this is what Lipstick means.

"I want to hunt treasures," I say bluntly.

Her slow, wide grin tells me this is the correct answer. "Of *course* you do," she says. "And that is exactly why we are going to help each other."

Of everything that she has said, it's the word "we" that sets my teeth on edge the most.

CHAPTER 20

NO WAY. FULL STOP.

DAD IS THE KING OF THE IDIOM. BUT HE IS NOT above reinterpreting a well-established and accepted idiom when it suits his needs. Take "A bird in the hand is worth two in the bush," one of his favorites. It means it is better to have a little of something than lots of nothing. However, Dad has used it to trip me up on plenty of occasions.

"Lola," he will explain with grave seriousness. "Sometimes the bird that you think you want is not actually the right bird. Leaving those birds in the bush will save you a lot of heartbreak down the line."

Confusing? Yes. I hear you. Living with my father some-

catastrophe? "The way I see it, if you want to level up, to play in the big kids' sandbox, to get post-camp glory and treasure-hunter privileges that will blow your mind, you'd better accept that things aren't always straight and narrow. There is always a compromise. Trust me."

Trust Lipstick? I might be able to accept the blurry edges of what is okay in the treasure-hunting world, but trusting Lipstick is one thing I will *never* do. Which leads me to a thought. Why *us*? She is not exactly a cheerleader for Team LJH and has a whole camp full of minions to use. Why not the Ms. Pac-Man crew? Or the kids in Cabin Six?

As if reading my mind, she sighs. "Believe me, I tried to work around you three. I considered the Cabin Six kids. But I miscalculated their abilities. They spilled salad dressing all over the clue I practically *hand delivered* them. All they had to do was spend some time figuring it out, but they were much more concerned with bragging rights and infighting. Not self-starters. And I also tried the boys in Cabin Two, but they were a hot mess. And don't even get me started on the group in Cabin Eight. They can barely get up in the morning on time. Or pick out a cereal to eat. If there is an opposite of action-oriented, they are it. And the misfits in One? So fragile! I thought that one with the freckles was going to cry every time I looked in her times requires mental gymnastics. But I'm thinking about those birds in the bush versus the one in my hand as I stand outside in the muggy night, mosquitoes sucking me dry, deep in a surreal conversation with my sworn enemy about how badly I want something that I want very badly. Some days just don't turn out like you planned.

I should reject this quid pro quo, this "You help me and I help you" offer from Lipstick and run very fast and far, but the prospect of successfully hunting the Helm, of redemption for the Pegasus disaster . . . I mean, *situation* . . . keeps me frozen in place, waiting to hear what she'll say next.

"I want you and your friends to hunt the Helm," she says. "Find it, acquire it, bring it back here, and I will happily applaud as you turn it over to the Task Force so they can stick it in their warehouse where it will get moldy."

There are so many things in that statement that require clarification. I start with the most glaring. "Hold on a sec. You would rather the Helm become the property of the government than end up with your nemesis?"

"I *never* said nemesis," Lipstick responds curtly. "I said *competitor*. There is a difference. Listen closely, kid. Whether you know it or not, you're in a hole, a deep one from the sound of it, on account of that total catastrophe with that necklace." Catastrophe? Disaster possibly, but direction. No grit. No tenacity. If time were not of the essence, I would send you all packing and bring in a full batch of new recruits. But alas, I don't have that luxury."

Lipstick squints at me. "Honestly, I have my doubts about you three. Your work is messy. Inelegant. Impulsive. Capturing the Stone of Istenanya smacked of dumb luck. But the clock is ticking and beggars can't be choosers. What is it going to be?"

My mouth is dry. My tongue sticks to my lips when I try to speak. I know Lipstick can't be trusted. Didn't she say things are seldom what they seem? What I don't know ought to scare me.

But I want to level up! I want to matter! I want to see Star and Fish, humbled and grateful, as we hand over the prize. I want to watch as they realize they never could have pulled this off without us. Because that will be *great*. Lipstick taps her foot impatiently.

"Well? I don't have all night for you to noodle this in that dizzy head of yours. It's win-win no matter how you look at it. Mostly."

"I shouldn't accept help without telling Jin and Hannah," I whisper.

"You have thirty seconds to say yes or no and then I outsource this project."

"How would you do that?"

"No concern of yours. Are you a leader or not? Leaders sometimes have to make choices for the team. Go ahead and stick their necks out and hope their heads don't get chopped off. Do you get what I'm saying?"

I do and I don't like any of it. There will be ramifications later for making any sort of deal with Lipstick, a price to pay that I don't yet recognize. Not to mention I should never put Jin and Hannah in the mix without even *asking* them. It's so wrong. But a mosquito buzzes my ear, and suddenly I say, "We're in. Tell me everything."

Lipstick grins and licks her lips like she is preparing to dine on my bones. "The Midnight Market is the only place to sell the Helm—"

"So it's *real*?" I interrupt. "This magical bazaar?"

Lipstick scoffs. "Of *course* it's real. But when and where it happens is a mystery. The organizers are quite . . . whimsical, if you will. They enjoy a bit of fun, and their idea of fun is watching everyone scramble around like blind moles in a complicated maze. The only semiconstant is that the market occurs in July."

"Once a year?" I ask. "That's it?"

Lipstick nods. "Blink and you miss it."

"And it's July now!"

"Wow," she says. "You really are as smart as they say." Was that necessary? I don't think so. "Now, my network, which remains extensive despite my new employer's attempts to dismantle it, informs me that the next Midnight Market will take place in New York City. That flyer you saw is the first clue I managed to get ahold of, and I'm working on uncovering additional details about when and where, but you must be ready to go at a moment's notice. As soon as we get specifics, we will snap into action." She is using the "we" word a *lot*. It makes me squirm. "And remember, Lola, this is between us. You and me. Tell *no one*. If you are caught, I will deny everything. Got it?"

I nod dumbly. And as Lipstick prepares to disappear into the inky black night, leaving me to wonder what just happened, she winks and says, "Welcome to my sandbox, Lola Benko."

CHAPTER 21

PARROTS AND MOOSE AND CROCODILES, OH MY

I SLEEP BADLY, DREAMING FOR SOME REASON OF angry crocodiles dragging me down to the depths of the sea and rolling me over and over until I drown. I saw a crocodile once in Australia. He was fifteen feet long with jagged rows of razor-sharp teeth that looked powerful enough to crush a small car. I have never been the same.

The third time I wake up, drenched in sweat, I call it good and keep my eyes open until the milky sun breaks through the darkness. It gives me plenty of time to consider what I have done. With a little bit of distance, the crocodiles actually seem like a better deal. Without consulting my team, I agreed to a deal with the *enemy*. Who does that?

I take a long time brushing my teeth, staring at my pale reflection in the mirror.

"You have to tell them," I say to myself. "Even if they get mad." But what if they decide they want to leave? Or don't like me anymore? What if I ruin everything?

Should have thought about that before you said yes, Lola. As Dad likes to say—I made my bed and now I get to lie in it.

I spit out a mouthful of toothpaste and creep back through the woods to our cabin. What are the chances there is a crocodile waiting in the shadows to drag me away? Not high? Hey, a girl can dream.

Jin and Hannah wake up ready to double down on our efforts to find the Midnight Market. They have ideas and theories, but I'm too distracted to listen, looking for a perfect moment to confess. That moment doesn't come.

At the crack of dawn, while filling my juice glass, I overhear a Cabin Six camper swear a parrot dive-bombed into their cabin last night and stole the flyer. His buddies dismiss him as sleep-deprived and delusional. If only they knew.

Plopping down in my seat, I bump my soggy bowl of granola and overturn it into my lap. Fabulous. This day is already a disaster and it has barely begun. But when I jump up, I realize there is something stuck to my butt. An envelope, to be exact. I peel it off and examine it.

Jin eyes me over a forkful of syrupy pancakes. "What's that?"

"A letter?" I reply, turning it over.

"Who writes letters?" Hannah asks. "Maybe it's hate mail from Ms. Pac-Man? We were for sure gaining on them in the ropes course yesterday."

"We for sure were *not*," Jin replies. "It could be an apology from Star and Fish, you know, for being jerks and siccing Moose on us and all."

"Right." Hannah snorts. "When pigs fly."

"Well, in this new magical world we live in, who is to say that pigs can't fly?" Jin snaps.

"How about I open it?" I suggest.

"Oh," says Jin. "Yeah."

Slowly, I peel back the envelope flap, suddenly anxious about what is inside. Will it explode? Will it bite me? Will it give me a rash? But it is simply an innocent piece of paper. My friends lean in.

"Well, that looks familiar," Hannah says, eyes bright.

"Yeah," Jin agrees. "Déjà vu." The page is a copy of the flyer we spent all night trying to decipher.

"Not exactly," I say. Because written along the bottom in a large sloping hand is:

Grand Central Terminal. New York City. 3 p.m. Thursday.

"It must be the time and place of the market," Jin says, breathless. "And that's today! But who is helping us?"

Hannah's grin covers her whole face. "It *has* to be Star and Fish. They have realized we are *indispensable* and they need us, and now they are helping us go rogue!"

No. That's not it at all. I should tell them about Lipstick right now. It's the perfect opportunity. But before I can open my mouth, Jin leaps out of his chair, fist pumping the air. "I *knew* they would see that we were the best kids for the job! I knew it! This feels *so* good." He practically glows with happiness. I have not seen him like this in a long time. In fact, I have not seen either of them this excited about *anything* since Pegasus. I cling to it.

And honestly, what would be gained from telling them about Lipstick? If we retrieve the Helm and get back on the Task Force, do the details of *how* matter? Dad says that when we use the ends to justify the means, it is often because the means are morally suspect. Is that what I'm doing?

"I have a question," Jin says. "How do we get out of here and to New York City in time to get to the market?"

Nothing like reality to rain on our parade. We are hundreds of miles from New York City. On an island. "We could steal a boat," Hannah suggests. "Or a car. Or call an Uber? Will they go that far?"

But Lipstick said she would help, so I wait to see what happens next. And what happens next is Moose.

"Uh-oh," Hannah says, squinting toward the cafeteria entrance. "Incoming." Moose, looking extra aggravated and sweaty for this early hour of the day, marches through the tables in our direction.

"He definitely knows about the phone," Jin whispers through clenched teeth. "We are going to get kicked out before we figure out a way to go rogue. How lame is that?"

Moose looms over our table. "I have been informed that your annoying comfort bird needs special medical care," he says, furious. "And that the specialized care can only be provided in New York City. And I have to get you three there *right away*." As if on cue, Zeus tips over and plays dead. He has always been a drama queen. Jin, catching on, strokes his downy feathers.

"It's devastating," Jin says, voice wobbly. "Poor little birdy."

Moose plants his palms on the table and leans in, toppling a carafe of syrup with his elbow. An amber river snakes toward the table's edge and drips to the floor. Moose does not notice, laser-focused on us. "Something stinks here and it's not the food."

"Oh, the food totally stinks," Hannah pipes up.

Moose throws his hands up in the air, exasperated. And remember, syrup is like an airborne contagion—once it is out of the bottle, there is no telling where it will end up. For example, Moose's eyebrow. "Every time I turn around, it's you kids and your problems. You have to go to the bathroom. Your bird is sick. I used to have a pretty good life and now look at it." The syrup clinging to his eyebrow gathers into a drip. "I thought I could handle this. Really. Well, come on! On your feet! We have to go to New York City."

Zeus, who has a short attention span, hops back to his feet and fluffs his feathers. Moose glares at us, death rays of displeasure that I feel right to the core of my being.

But none of this changes the facts. We have our ride to New York City.

We are *hunting* the Helm of Darkness.

CHAPTER 22

STAR AND FISH TAKE A FIELD TRIP

STAR: *That whole experience was deeply traumatizing. I may never recover.*

FISH: *36 hours of flying is a lot.*

STAR: *Especially stowed away in a cargo plane. With no food! No water! Practically no heat! I still can't feel my toes!*

FISH: *You are being a big baby. I know it was uncomfortable, but we are in stealth mode. Do you even know what that means?*

STAR: *Yes. The trip was still awful.*

FISH: *Fine. It was awful. But it was necessary. No one knows we are here in New York. It will take the Task Force at least a few days to figure out we are missing from Siberia, and by that point we will have the Helm.*

STAR: *I hope you are right.*

FISH: *I am.*

STAR: *Well, okay, I guess . . . and are you ever going to tell me how you got the clue to the location of the Midnight Market?*

FISH: *It's classified.*

STAR: *We are partners. Our level of clearance is identical.*

FISH: *Classified by me, I mean.*

STAR: *So you just don't want to tell me?*

FISH: *I might. One day. For now, you have to trust me. Information is on a need-to-know basis, and you don't need to know.*

STAR: *Oh, that's great. Is that why you are making me sit in a different train car than you? So you don't accidentally tell me things I don't need to know?*

FISH: *What? No! Remember the stealth-mode thing? We need to take precautions. Getting caught is not an option.*

STAR: *Yeah. Yeah. Whatever. My train car smells like tuna fish. I'm just saying.*

FISH: *You will love me when you get to surf the Mediterranean.*

STAR: *Do you really think you can pull this off? I mean, do you really think we can pull this off?*

FISH: *Definitely. And once we bag the Helm, the world is our oyster.*

STAR: *I don't like oysters. It's like eating snot.*

FISH: *Thank you for that lovely image.*

STAR: *It's true.*

FISH: *Let's not talk about oysters ever again.*

STAR: *You brought them up!*

FISH: *Never mind. Moving on. When our train gets to New York City, we have to head directly for Grand Central Terminal.*

STAR: *Why? More trains? Are we ever going to get where we are going?*

FISH: *The answers you seek are written in the stars.*

STAR: *I really hate it when you talk cryptic. It makes me nervous. Plus, I have no idea what you mean.*

FISH: *Don't worry. It will all make sense soon.*

STAR: *Whatever. I'm finding another seat that's not so smelly. Maybe there is a train car that smells like cinnamon buns? That would be better.*

FISH: *I have no response to that.*

CHAPTER 23

THE URBAN JUNGLE

THE PROBLEM WITH GETTING TO NEW YORK CITY is that the tin-can plane is currently unavailable due to the pilot's mysterious disappearance in Greenland. Moose's only choice is to drive us there in a rickety minivan with shoddy air-conditioning that is as loud as a jet engine. As you can imagine, this does not make him happy.

"I must have been very bad in a past life," he mutters, barely audible, to himself. "There is no other explanation. I really have to think about my future."

It's 347 miles from Camp Timber Wolf in the Thousand Islands to Grand Central Terminal in New York City. The GPS estimates it will take us seven hours to complete the journey. This is a long time to be squished in a car that smells like bug repellent and sweat. Within the first five miles, Moose points out that showering is not actually complicated. "All you do is stand under the water," he grumbles. "Maybe you kids should try it sometime."

In response, we roll down the windows and let in the hot, humid air. Zeus fluffs his feathers in the wind, the parrot version of a dog sticking his head out the window to catch the breeze. The air is tinged with the smell of fertilizer. There are a lot of cows up here in northern New York.

I'd like to say I get right to planning what we will do to find the Midnight Market when we arrive at Grand Central Terminal, because I have all sorts of brilliant ideas floating around in my head that I cannot wait to share. But instead I am lulled to sleep by the rhythm of the road, my late-night clandestine meeting with Lipstick finally catching up with me. Scrunched down in my seat, chin lolling on chest, snoring, drooling, and generally being gross, I nap for at least a hundred miles. My limbs feel loose and twitchy, and I keep snapping my head back to center as it tilts awkwardly to one side. I'm completely uncomfortable, but my body refuses to surface to full consciousness to fix the situation. I'm just too tired.

Hannah's face is buried in a book while Jin stares out the

window at the densely forested scenery outside. New York has a lot of trees to go along with the cows. Zeus, perched on Jin's shoulder, keeps in character, dramatically rolling his eyes and loudly gagging every half hour so Moose remembers he's gravely ill. Each time, Jin soothes him and whispers that everything will be okay. Zeus could not be happier.

Eventually, I regain consciousness, yawning so widely my jaw feels like it might unhinge. Outside, there's a lake every mile. Water, trees, cows. Hannah stares at me over the cover of her novel. "It lives," she says.

"Barely," I groan, trying to work out the kink in my neck.

"Are you ready to talk about what we are going to do when we get there?" Hannah asks. Jin turns away from the window. Now they both stare at me. They want the plan. Which I don't have. Because I was napping. And drooling.

"Does anyone have water?" I ask, stalling. Jin hands me a water bottle. I take a long swig. I swish it around in my mouth. I take another. It has to be a good plan to make up for previous bad plans, and I'm feeling the pressure. *Come on, Lola. Think!*

Hannah leans across me to Jin. "She has *no* idea what we are going to do when we get there," she says flatly.

Jin studies me. "Is that true?" he asks.

"I'm working on it," I mutter. The problem is I have very little to work *with*. A time, a destination, and that's it. Does

it mean the market will take place at three o'clock in Grand Central Terminal? That doesn't seem likely. It's crowded there. Maybe that is the time the next clue will be revealed? Or is it something else entirely that we haven't even considered? And there is *no way* I ask Moose if he happens to know anything. It's enough to make a girl want to go back to sleep.

But this is no time to panic. I take a deep breath. Back when I used to be in the art-thieving business, I always started planning a heist with some small piece of information. For example, I saw a valuable ballerina sculpture in a local San Francisco art magazine and worked out a plan to steal it from there. Of course, that ended up with me in the emergency room getting stitches in my butt, but that is not the point here. I started with next to nothing and soon had a full-fledged plan of action even if the ultimate result was failure. I remind myself this is not that different. But I will skip the failure part.

"So here's what we do," I say, my voice masked by the struggling air-conditioning. "We go to the terminal. We look around."

Hannah raises a sharp eyebrow. "*That's* the plan?"

"It's an *evolving* plan," I say a little defensively. "We can call it the information-gathering stage of the plan."

"We go there, we look around, we decide what to do

next?" Jin asks. "Just, you know, clarifying."

"Yup. That about sums it up."

"Great," Jin says with a wide grin. "Of *course* it will work." When I realize he's not actually being sarcastic, I smile back. Hannah rolls her eyes.

"Okay, I guess," she says. "But can we try to make it fun? I'm bored. Like, really *really* bored. Road trips are the worst. Just driving and driving and more driving. Plus, the best character in my book died." She tosses the half-finished novel over her shoulder in disgust. "Stupid author."

"We will do our best to make it fun," I say solemnly. A bored Hannah is a potentially dangerous Hannah, to herself and others.

Slowly the scenery begins to change. The trees recede and tall buildings appear on the horizon. The road becomes decidedly bumpier and full of potholes. As we roll down the east side of the Hudson River, I notice a few sailboats and a big freighter on the wide waterway. The steep cliffs on the far side are actually New Jersey, which looks full of trees like New York. I wonder if they have cows.

The massive George Washington Bridge looms overhead as we weave our way down the road. Yellow taxis zoom in and out of lanes without a care in the world. Construction cranes dot the skyline. A near miss with a battered limousine demonstrates that Moose can curse in multiple languages.

I have been in New York City a few times. The last time was when my father urgently needed to visit the American Museum of Natural History on Central Park West to talk to an archaeologist about a pressing matter, although he was vague on the details.

"Important things," he said, dismissing my questions. "Stuff that must be discussed."

We flew eleven long hours from Casablanca, Morocco, to JFK Airport, where we jumped into a taxi so my dad could meet the scholar for a discussion of "stuff and things" over a quick cup of coffee. The caffeine barely had a chance to take effect before we immediately reversed the journey. When I asked Dad to explain why he couldn't have had his important conversation over the phone, he waved me off.

"Sometimes you need to see a person's face," he explained, which was really no explanation at all. And he did not take kindly to my detailed description of the wonders of FaceTime or Zoom, nor my insistence that in certain situations an electronic face is as good as a real one. But when we got out of the taxi in front of the museum, I remember very *clearly* Dad taking a deep inhale and grinning. "New York City is full of magic," he said with a wink.

Guess he wasn't kidding.

CHAPTER 24

RUN

WE WATCH THE STREET NUMBERS DESCEND, AND we are blowing by 140th Street when Moose's cell phone rings. His ringtone is the theme music from Darth Vader because *of course* it is! He presses the phone to his ear as we strain to hear him over the noise. Brows furrowed, he chews his thumbnail while nodding and grunting. Sliding off my sweat-soaked seat, I wedge into the small space behind the driver. If I crane my neck at a very awkward angle, I can actually hear the caller's voice. Oh, and it sounds familiar. I glance back at Jin and Hannah and make fish lips. They giggle. Great.

Fish, I mouth. These are the words I distinctly hear:

"parrot," "trick," "get rid of," "dump," "Macombs Dam Bridge," "hurry," "remove." And you know what I think? Sure, you do. The parrot is a trick. Get rid of the kids by dumping them off the bridge. Hurry up and remove the problem.

Moose jerks the wheel, flying off the exit and heading east. I wiggle out of the tight space and back to my damp seat to relay the intel. Jin and Hannah agree with my assessment that we are about to be pitched off a bridge into the Harlem River and left to drown. As appealing as a swim is right now, this won't work.

"You didn't happen to bring that cell phone, did you?" I ask Jin.

"No!" he snaps. "You guys told me I wasn't even allowed to *think* about it."

Okay. That's true. But also unfortunate.

"We need to jump out of the van," Hannah says, matter-of-fact.

"It's *moving*," Jin points out. "We could conk Moose on the head."

"And then the whole van crashes and Fish gets her wish," Hannah objects.

They both face me. "Well? Now what?"

But this time I have a plan. "Remember how Moose

banned accidentally barfing in his car because you can never really get it clean?" I ask.

Hannah grins. "Oh yeah. Right. Can I do it? Please?"

I nod. "Sure. Go for it."

"Excuse me?" Jin says. "What exactly are we doing?"

"Watch."

Hannah closes her eyes, takes a deep inhale, and produces a garbled, choking scream that so startles Moose he practically careens off the road anyway, which is what we wanted to avoid. But too late now. Hannah is in the zone. She gags and heaves and buckles at the waist, clutching her stomach and moaning.

"What is going on back there?" Moose glances anxiously in the rearview mirror.

"Hannah is carsick," I yell, sounding as desperate as possible. "She's going to puke! You better pull over!"

Moose does not even hesitate. He does not question the sincerity of Hannah's carsickness for a second. The van cuts across two lanes of traffic, inciting the ire of our fellow travelers, and stops hard on the narrow shoulder.

"When the door opens," I whisper, "grab your backpack and run."

"Run!" Zeus squawks. Wonderful. That bird is going to get us all killed. Gently, Jin wraps a hand around Zeus to keep him from fluttering away. Hannah continues to gag as Moose jumps from the driver's seat and darts around the minivan to pull open the door.

Three. Two. One. Go! We rush him like a rogue wave, a flurry of arms and legs and feathers.

"Come back here, you kids!" he bellows. "You are going in that river! That is final!"

No *way* we are going in that river. "Run!" I yell. We dart from the van down the gravelly shoulder and into a tangle of trees that seem out of place in the urban landscape. I can hear Moose's labored breathing behind me. He might be strong, but he lacks endurance. Coming up behind Jin, I give him a shove to the left around . . . tombstones? Worn smooth by years of rain, names faded, but yes, we are in a cemetery. Well, that's creepy. But it's also a little like running around inside a pinball machine. Moose can't keep up, and soon we lose him in the maze of what a sign indicates is Trinity Church Cemetery. Ducking down behind a large headstone, breathless, we can barely speak. Our limbs feel like rubber.

"Hey," Jin wheezes, glancing around. "Is this where Alexander Hamilton is buried?"

"No," I gasp. "He's downtown at the Trinity Church Wall Street graveyard. Different place."

"Maybe we work that in somehow?" he asks. "I'm a fan."

"Sure," Hannah says. "First, run for our lives. Second, a Hamilton tour of New York."

"Jeez," Jin replies. "It was just a thought. Why did Fish want us thrown off a bridge? I thought they were the ones enabling this whole fiasco."

This would be the perfect time to tell them about Lipstick and how *she* is actually our benefactor. But we are still panting from the running-for-our-lives part of the day, and it doesn't seem right.

"I don't know," I say quietly. After a few moments, it's clear that Moose is not following us. We seem to have successfully escaped. Which is really great. What's not so great is that we are far away from Grand Central Terminal and the clock is ticking. I tap my watch face.

"We have to move fast if we have any hope of getting there in time," I say. As we snake our way out of the cemetery and back to the streets, we argue over whether we have enough money for cab fare or the bus. The answer is a positive maybe. We head down a wide avenue as I anxiously glance at my watch.

"Stop doing that," Hannah says. "Time is going to happen whether you watch it or not."

"You sound like Professor Benko," Jin says, elbowing her.

"Who sounds like me?"

And suddenly, out of nowhere, there is Dad blocking the sidewalk, his hair long and shaggy, his leather jacket covered in a fine layer of what is most likely Peruvian dust. I hate to admit it, but I'm rendered speechless, something that almost never happens.

"Professor Benko!" Jin throws his arms around my father while Dad pulls Hannah and me in for a hug.

"What are you doing here?" Hannah asks.

"You're s-supposed to be hunting diamonds," I stutter.

"Well, it's a long story." We don't have time for a long story. We barely have time for this conversation.

"Dad," I interrupt. "We need to be at Grand Central in, like, twenty minutes. It's urgent."

Dad's face gets serious. "Got it. You can give me details en route." He steps to the edge of the sidewalk and throws up an arm, and as if by magic, a green cab pulls to the curb.

"Air-conditioning." Jin sighs with pleasure.

"Jin." Zeus sighs with pleasure.

"What is going on?" Dad asks, not sighing with pleasure.

"You first," I insist. I don't know how Dad is going to react to us being here rather than tucked away at Camp Timber Wolf as we are supposed to be.

"As you can imagine, Irma was quite upset to find that Zeus had gone AWOL," Dad begins. "She suspected that his love for Jin got in the way of his reasoning."

"You're assuming that Zeus *has* reasoning to begin with," I interject.

"Mean Lola," Zeus spits.

Dad waves us off. "No matter. Fortunately, he is chipped."

"The bird?" Hannah asks.

"Indeed," Dad replies. "Irma does not mess around when it comes to avian safety."

"Chipped?" Zeus squawks.

"For your own good," Dad says.

"Chipped?" Zeus repeats, this time at volume eleven. I don't think he likes the idea. Before Dad can further explain, Zeus tucks his head under his wing and refuses to come out. Great. Now Zeus is having a snit.

"Oh, Zeus," Dad says with a sigh. "You do like dramatic effect, don't you? In any case, Irma found Zeus at camp and asked that I go there immediately to retrieve him. She did not want to make a big deal out of it in case it got you three in trouble. But when I woke this morning, fully intending to fly up to camp, I saw that Zeus was in fact headed here, to New York City. So I followed the tracker, and now here we are. But *why* are we here, kids?"

"We're hunting the Helm of Darkness," I say, my mouth dry and gritty. Dad's eyes flash hot for a moment, but he gets it under control.

"And how did this come to pass?" he asks patiently.

As I explain, he nods and tilts his head and mutters things like "interesting" and "unusual" and "rogue is never a good choice." At the end of my tale, he goes quiet, which makes me sweat even more than I'm already sweating.

"While I understand why you did what you did," he says finally, "I rather wish you'd stayed at camp."

I hang my head. "I know."

"But I'd be lying if I said I never broke the rules," Dad continues, "so I'm willing to reserve judgment for the moment. And as long as we are here, we might as well see it through. The Helm is a good find. Besides, I haven't been to a Midnight Market in ages, and they are jolly good fun, as long as they don't know I'm there. As you can imagine, Task Force treasure hunters are not exactly welcome. But you will never see anything like it in your life."

"Wait," Jin asks, eyes wide. "Professor Benko, does this mean you are going to treasure hunt *with* us?"

Dad chuckles. "Think of me as an advisor of sorts. There

will be no glory for you three if the perception is that I did the work. I want you to proceed as if I were not here. I will, however, pay cab fare and buy pizza slices."

"This is going to be wild," Hannah says. "Tell us more about the market."

"Well, it's been around for as long as magical objects have existed, which is forever. The story goes that it has changed management a few times down through the ages, people dying and new folks taking over. And try as we might, we have never been able to figure out who is in charge at any given moment. But oh, to attend the Midnight Market." Dad looks suddenly wistful, as if remembering a time from long ago and well lost. He shakes it off and smiles. "A person is never quite the same."

Something about his words puts me on high alert, my senses heightened. But I push that aside and focus on the fact that I'm treasure hunting with my *father*. How cool is that?

CHAPTER 25

IN A CRUNCH? STOP FOR CUPCAKES.

THE CAR AND PEDESTRIAN TRAFFIC IN MIDTOWN Manhattan is spectacular. The streets are gridlocked, and people fill every square inch of sidewalk space. Clueless tourists gaze up at the towering real estate while locals plow them aside, like ducks through water. Big red touring buses crowd the curb, and taxis line up to fetch passengers. Several blocks from the station, Dad pays the fare and we run. On the plus side, it's New York, so no one looks twice at the parrot riding along on Jin's shoulder, squawking and bellowing.

A group of ruddy-cheeked German tourists sweeps us up in their wake, dragging us toward the 42nd Street entrance to the terminal. Disentangling ourselves, we slip through the heavy doors and into a blast of chilled air. The terminal is layered in smells—a fine bakery, sweaty feet, an electrical fire, moldy newspaper, French fries. To one side of the grand entrance hall are thriving food stalls, and to the other is a museum exhibit featuring glass cases of the fancy dresses of a rich-and-famous someone who had *lots* of fancy dresses. Jin wants to stop and admire the tulle and sequins and satin, but this is no sightseeing tour. I urge him on.

"Come on," I say. "We don't have much time." A short walk and the Main Concourse opens before us. Across the massive hall are numbered platform entrances to the trains. To the right side of the hall, wide dramatic stairs lead up and away to additional levels of the station. Dead ahead is the bedazzled information booth and iconic clock. Thousands of people move like a rushing river, densely packed and yet seemingly oblivious of one another, focused entirely on some future destination. This cannot be where the Midnight Market takes place. It's too crowded.

"I don't think we will be shopping for magical objects here," Hannah says, echoing my thoughts.

"Of course not," Dad says. "This is certainly the location

for another clue. The Midnight Market organizers dearly love landmarks." I glance around the packed terminal, wondering how many other people are here for the same reason we are.

"But where?" Jin asks, throwing his hands up. Grand Central covers forty-eight *acres*. That's roughly thirty-six football fields' worth of space. There is a very good chance that if something happens at three o'clock, we will miss it because we are in the wrong place. I dig in my shorts pocket for the crumpled flyer. Hannah snatches it from my hand.

It's the exact moment my father clutches my arm. His jaw is tight and his face suddenly pale. "Lola," he says. "Do you hear that sound?"

"Huh?" I hear a lot of sounds. This place is mobbed.

"Like tinkling bells? Like breaking glass? Like if a butterfly were flapping crystal wings?"

I look at my dad. What a strange thing to ask. But okay. I concentrate. Bells. Breaking glass. Crystal butterfly wings. And I catch just a note of it high-pitched above the general din. "Maybe?"

"But it cannot be," my father whispers. "It *cannot*."

"Dad?"

My father takes me by the shoulders. "Lola, continue on. I will rendezvous with you shortly."

"Wait! What is going on? When?" But he's gone, swimming through the tide of people toward whatever he thinks he heard. What on earth is this about?

My friends, bent over the flyer, miss this entire exchange. Hannah glances up to see the back of my father's head as he vanishes into the crowd. "Where is he going?" she asks.

"To get doughnuts?" Jin adds hopefully.

"No doughnuts," I say. "He just . . . thought he heard something weird. I think? Anyway, he said he'd catch up, and we have work to do. What are we missing on the flyer? There has to be *something*." We plunge deeper into the terminal, and as we pass the information desk, I swipe a map. But nothing on it sparks a connection. Did Lipstick get it wrong? Where is Dad when we really could use his help? Hopelessness begins to seep in right at the moment when Jin abruptly stops, and I crash into him. He, in turn, bursts out laughing. "Not funny," I say. "Not funny at all."

"Duh," he says, eyes tilted skyward. "The *ceiling*." I follow his gaze and . . . oh . . . wow. Twelve stories above unfolds an aquamarine sky upon which the constellations of Orion, Taurus, and Gemini float in yellow starry relief. The expanse is enormous. I hold up the tattered flyer to see if the stars align.

"It doesn't match any of the constellations," Hannah

says, puzzled. "I checked them. Double-checked them. Triple-checked them!"

"Maybe it's not specific?" I suggest.

The giant clock is about to strike three. The concourse is a cacophony of sound, voices, pounding feet, train engines. The dull roar makes it hard to think. "The 3:02 express train to White Plains is now leaving from the lower level, track number 110," booms a voice. We stare at the ceiling. Nothing happens.

"What do we do?" asks Jin.

"Do you see anything?" asks Hannah.

"Nope," Jin replies.

I glance at my watch. 3:01. Now what? But then Jin points. "Look!" A single star in one of the constellations is suddenly aglow, illuminated by a dozen bright lights. As the station is flooded with afternoon sun, it would be impossible to see if you weren't already looking.

"It's the Northern Fly!" Hannah shouts, pumping her fist in the air. "The constellation that got fired!"

Great! But what does it *mean*? A bead of sweat rolls down my back. The lights stop flickering, and the ceiling returns to normal.

"That was kind of interesting," Jin says. "But how does it help us find the Midnight Market?"

A detail nudges me, and a thought is glued together. The terminal *map*. I hold it right up to my nose.

"Northern Fly," I mutter.

"What is she doing?" Jin asks Hannah.

"Talking to herself," Hannah replies.

"Here! Look!" I jab the spot on the map labeled *Northern Fly Cupcakes*.

Jin grins. "Cupcakes. Rad."

"Cupcakes!" Zeus hollers, waking from his snooze. Food always gets his attention.

"It *has* to be connected," I say. "Right?" Plus, cupcakes are whimsical by their very nature, and Lipstick said the organizers were whimsical.

"Finally, something real!" Hannah yelps, and takes off for the lower-level food court.

"Hungry!" shrieks Zeus, loud enough to attract the attention of a school group. The kids "oh" and "ah" over him, and he preens like royalty. That bird is a show-off.

"You have to wait," I tell Zeus. "Your belly is not priority one right now."

Jin strokes Zeus's ruffled feathers. "It's okay," he says soothingly. "We will get you a snack soon. I promise." Boy, Zeus is getting so spoiled he might actually be ruined.

Northern Fly Cupcakes is a small kiosk located across

from track 102. Inside the glass display case is a dazzling array of beautiful cupcakes, each one more delightful than the next. They wink with sparkling sprinkles and swirling clouds of creamy frosting. My teeth ache just looking at them.

Behind the counter is a man with a long beard and a red bandanna covering his bald head. His beady eyes are dark and hooded. Unsmiling, he cleans the glass display case while flexing thick forearms covered in bright tattoos. But instead of snarling tigers or creepy snakes or whatever, the tattoos are all images of sweets. There are Hershey's Kisses, cake slices topped with whipped cream, lollipops, and cookies. Mmmmmm. Yum.

Stop it right now, Lola! Focus!

Right. On it. The man sees us standing before him but doesn't acknowledge our existence. I inhale sharply and stride forward, unsure of what I'm supposed to be looking for but with no time left to be cautious.

"Excuse me?" I ask. "Do you have any cupcakes?" The man glances at me, at the cupcake display, and back at me. He doesn't say "duh," but that is what he's thinking. "Maybe a *special* one called the Midnight or the Market or something?"

His eyebrows shoot up. He stops cleaning the glass and

tosses the dirty towel over his shoulder. He narrows his gaze. "Is that a parrot?" he asks.

Jin swallows hard and inches forward, like the Cowardly Lion in *The Wizard of Oz*. "Yes," he says, his voice quaking. "A parrot. Absolutely."

Zeus knows he is the subject of conversation, and this perks him right up. He's a diva, as I've said. "Cupcake!" he squawks. "Immediately!" The man's eyes go wide. This rude parrot is going to ruin everything! But instead, the man breaks into a wide grin. His beady eyes grow warm.

"I do so love me a talking parrot," he says quietly, almost to himself. "Do you like carrot cake, little bird?"

Does Zeus like carrot cake? What a question! Zeus is basically an avian goat. He will eat anything, even shoelaces. The man carefully extracts a perfect cupcake wrapped in pink paper and holds it out to Jin, who takes the precious offering tentatively.

Zeus, however, does not respect the presentation of beautiful food. He just wants to eat it. Like a lunatic, he launches himself into the cupcake, beak first, and tears it apart. I fully expect the tattooed baker to pound us with those massive forearms, but he cracks up.

"A talking bird with taste," he says, wiping his eyes. "Here. You might need this. You have a job ahead of you."

He holds out a napkin. Oh, we're going to need more than one. We're going to need a whole stack. And possibly a hose. Bits of frosting fly everywhere. What a mess. But as I attempt to wipe down Zeus's greasy feathers with the napkin, I realize it is not a napkin at all. It's a flyer, much like the one Lipstick gave us, except with different images.

When I look behind the counter for the man, he's gone.

CHAPTER 26

FOLLOW THE CLUES

THE FLYER IS SMEARED WITH FROSTING, BUT I manage to pull it away before Zeus pecks it full of holes. The design includes clouds, trees, and train tracks that appear to be floating in an iridescent sky.

"The last flyer had a bunch of stars," Hannah says, brows furrowed. "And it was about the landmark ceiling in Grand Central. Professor Benko said they liked landmarks, right?"

"They have flying train tracks in New York City?" Jin asks. "Wild."

"You are being literal," Hannah replies with a grimace. "Be abstract."

"Got it." But he's not being either. Instead, he's cleaning the bird, who is covered in brightly colored frosting and sprinkles.

We study the flyer some more. Are we meant to check every track in Grand Central? With sixty-seven tracks, that could take some time. Or maybe it's a subway station? There are 472 of those. That would also take a while.

We scrounge up some money and buy a black-and-white cookie to share while we walk around the station searching for inspiration or my dad. We find neither. We stand on a really long line to use the bathrooms. We scan book covers at a bookstore and eyeball giant lollipops at a candy vendor. We watch a lady yell and curse at her exploding suitcase. Eventually, we end up out front, by the main entrance, our backs to the hot concrete wall as we watch people stream by.

"Did he say where he was going?" Jin asks.

"I think he saw someone he thought he knew," I reply. "But it was weird, like he was freaked out."

"I guess we wait for him?" Hannah asks.

"I guess?" But it's four o'clock now and the Midnight Market happens tonight, with or without us.

A flushed man wearing a sandwich-board sign advertising Big Red Bus Tours shoves a handful of brochures in my hands. "Discounted tours right here! See the sights!

Visit the museums! Live the dream! Twenty percent off! Full AC! Thrill of a lifetime!"

I'm about to toss the brochures in the trash when Hannah suddenly grabs one. "Wait!"

And there it is. The floating-train-track image, printed in bright colors. "What the heck is the High Line?" I ask. Fortunately, the brochure has all the answers.

"The High Line is a 1.45-mile-long elevated linear park," Hannah reads aloud, "created on the former New York Central Railroad spur on the west side of Manhattan in New York City. It's a 'rails to trails' thing. You know, taking abandoned train tracks and turning them into paths for biking and walking and stuff. It's not that far from here. We could walk to it easy."

"But what about Professor Benko?" Jin asks.

"He specifically said continue on, didn't he?" Hannah replies. I nod. "Well, that means we go!"

Jin looks unsure, but Hannah is right—our next step involves this park floating above the city. "My dad will find us. Remember the bird tracker? Let's go."

"Are you sure?" Jin asks. "This feels weird."

"Jin," I say in all seriousness. "If you lived a moment in my life before I ended up in San Francisco, you would not find any of this weird. Believe me."

Of course, the last time my father mysteriously vanished, things went seriously sideways and the entire world was at risk. I certainly hope we are not traveling down that path again. There is only so much a girl can be expected to take when it comes to disappearing fathers.

CHAPTER 27

STAR AND FISH CATCH A BREAK

STAR: *Do you think Moose did the . . . you know . . . thing?*

FISH: *He confirmed he did. I got a text from him. Coast is clear of annoying brats. Thank goodness.*

STAR: *But a bridge? Was that necessary?*

FISH: *We do what we have to do. Are you turning chicken again?*

STAR: *No! But it would help if I knew what we were doing in Grand Central Terminal and what I was supposed to be looking for.*

FISH: *You will know it when you see it. Pay attention.*

STAR: *All I see are people.*

FISH: *That's because Grand Central is one of the busiest train stations in the world. Are you still at your lookout post?*

STAR: *Yes. I'm standing on the staircase, pretending to text. Actually, I am texting.*

FISH: *Keep your eyes open.*

STAR: *They are. And you don't need to tell me that every two seconds. I'm not twelve.*

FISH: *Fine. What do you see?*

STAR: *I told you already! People! Can I take five minutes to get a cup of coffee? All this travel has made me tired. My eyeballs feel like sticky, itchy marbles in my head. It's not okay.*

FISH: *Quit whining! Being a treasure hunter means you never get tired! No coffee breaks! Marbles open!*

STAR: *I'm starting to regret agreeing to this boondoggle. Was Siberia that bad? I mean, yes, it's cold and everything is frozen, including the residents, but still, I was starting to adjust.*

FISH: *I cannot believe what I am hearing. From the moment you stepped foot on Siberian soil, all you did was complain, complain, complain.*

STAR: *Did not!*

FISH: *Did too!*

FISH: *Are you giving me the silent treatment? Grow up already. And remember, you will change your tune when you are on the beach. Eyes on the prize.*

STAR: *You are obsessed with eyes.*

FISH: *Do you see anything?*

STAR: *No! What am I looking for?*

FISH: *I already told you! The first clue to the location of the Midnight Market will be revealed here in Grand Central.*

STAR: *You are aware that this place is huge? Can you be more specific?*

FISH: *I wish.*

STAR: *So that is a no?*

FISH: *Oh wait! I see something! She's headed for the 42nd Street exit. Silver hair. White dress. Bracelets. She looks so familiar. Where have I seen her before? I don't know, but it has to mean something! Meet me down by the information booth clock. It's time to move.*

STAR: *Thank goodness. Can I grab a coffee first?*

FISH: *NO!*

STAR: *Jeez. Okay. Relax. I'm coming.*

CHAPTER 28

DEPLOY THE PARROT

IT IS SEVENTEEN BLOCKS FROM GRAND CENTRAL Terminal to the High Line entrance on 34th Street. Thirty-five minutes of walking and I'm so sweaty you'd think I took a dip in the Hudson River, which is right there in front of us. We are about as far west as we can go on Manhattan Island without falling in the water. During the walk, Zeus, riding along with Jin, worries a clump of feathers under his right wing, nipping and pecking at it until we have words.

"Is this because of stress?" I ask. Parrots are prone to repetitive self-harm when they are stressed. "Are you anxious?" He blinks at me a few times as if I am an idiot and returns to pecking his bird armpit. Okay. Maybe not that.

"Is there still frosting stuck under there? Or sprinkles? If you didn't eat like such a maniac, maybe this wouldn't happen." He pirouettes on Jin's shoulder and shakes his tail feathers at me, and I bet you know what that means.

"Zeus." I grab him, intending to take a look at the spot, but my fingers come away with a smudge of blood. "You did *not*."

Oh, but he did! Cocking his head to one side, he spits a tiny silver disc into the gutter, where it immediately slides down a drainage opening. No! "You guys," I say. "Zeus is no longer chipped." Can parrots smile? Maybe.

"But how is Professor Benko going to find us?" Hannah yells.

"Zeus tired," the bird mutters, and noses his way into Jin's backpack for a nap. Well, this part of our hunt is off to a roaring good start. I should have stuffed Zeus in a FedEx box and mailed him back to San Francisco the moment I realized he was a stowaway. But now it's too late.

"Come on," I say, resigned. "This way."

The entrance to the High Line is a curved walkway leading up to the old elevated train tracks. The Hudson River glitters in the sun, and sailboats dot the water. The main path is about forty feet wide, full of plants and trees, like a garden oasis floating above the chaos. Once again, we have no idea what we are looking for. At least this is something we are getting used to.

"Do we wander around like usual?" Jin asks.

Hannah gulps from her water bottle and looks around. "Keep your eyes open," she says, "and look for anything, you know, *weird*."

"This is New York City," I reply. "Everything is weird. They do it on purpose."

Zeus pops his head out of Jin's backpack, cheery and refreshed after his cupcake and power nap. Surveying the scene, he's completely delighted. "Ohhhhhh," he coos, eye-balling the trees and blooming flowers.

"No running away," I say sharply. "Or flying away. Or whatever." We do not have time in the schedule to search for a lost bird, and without the chip he is a free agent.

"Why do you keep ordering him around?" Jin asks. "He can't understand you."

"That's what you think," I say. "Let's get going." It's close to five o'clock. We need to make progress. The Midnight Market is not going to find us.

The High Line is pretty but not exactly *fun*. "So many trees," Hannah groans as we trudge down the path. She's unimpressed by the fact that we are basically a few stories off the ground, where trees don't normally grow. "This is the kind of place parents bring kids on vacation when they want to torture them."

"We went to Disneyland once," Jin offers. "I waited two hours for a four-minute ride. *That* was torture."

Dad and I didn't vacation like normal people because we were always somewhere exotic or strange to begin with. And Dad is not the vacationing type. He can't sit on a beach, reading a book with his toes dipped in the water. Or spend an afternoon making sandcastles. He's much too restless.

"You guys!" Hannah shouts suddenly. "Look!"

Jin and I pull to an abrupt stop and follow the direction where Hannah points. "What is it?" I ask, my pulse leaping. Has she found the clue we've been searching for?

"More *trees*," she says with a sly smile.

"Don't do that again," Jin fumes. "This is serious."

"Believe me, I know that," Hannah shoots back. "Seriously *dull*." As it turns out, adrenaline junkies are crabby when things get slow.

"Walk faster," I instruct. "We have a lot of ground to cover."

We fan out, me and Hannah on the far edges of the path and Jin straight down the middle, scanning everything as we go. Which is not easy. The High Line is teeming with tourists. They stop and gawk and point and block our way and talk too much. We pass a fifteen-foot sculpture of a telescope made out of metal. I bet it's valuable but much too big for my backpack. We pass a food vendor selling homemade ice cream. Jin eyes the cart longingly. "Don't get distracted," I say, more to myself than to him.

"Sure. Right." But his gaze stays glued to the cart of frozen treats. Dad calls New York an "empty pocket" city because it's expensive and you inevitably leave with no money in your pocket. Our mistake was *starting* with empty pockets.

Focus, Lola! Pining for ice cream is not going to find you the Midnight Market!

Hannah is right about the trees. There are a lot of them. And plants and sculptures and a big lawn section completely covered in sweaty bodies, lounging on the grass. We pass a water feature and oversize wooden deck chairs. But no signs of the Midnight Market or anything else that might be a clue. I push back on the creeping despair, but it is persistent and stubborn and heavy. This would not be so bad if it were fifteen degrees cooler. I'm getting a sunburn.

Buildings frame the High Line, apartments close enough we can look directly into them. I imagine it is nicer to have a garden right outside your window than train tracks, even if the garden is crowded with strangers peering in on you like you are a zoo animal. Through one window, we see a woman lying on a couch reading a book, an oscillating fan on a stool next to her. Another window reveals a guy doing yoga. He's twisted up like a pretzel. I'm about to suggest a water break when Hannah grabs my arm.

"What?" I ask. "More trees?"

"Yes. But also, *that*." She points into an apartment, partially obscured by enormous ceramic planters, as tall as I am. Painted on the wall, six feet high and three feet wide and clear as day, are the fancy calligraphed emerald-green initials *MM* nestled in a bloodred braided circle.

I press into the railing, leaning as close to the apartment as I can without falling off the High Line. From this vantage point, it's clear the symbol is actually a giant poster tacked to the wall. The room is empty save for a plastic beach pail in the middle of the floor. Dangling from the ceiling is an unglamorous light fixture that resembles an upside-down flying saucer. The large window facing us is open just a crack. We need whatever is in that pail. I guess we go in there and get it?

"I can do this," I say confidently.

Jin looks horrified. "Who do you think you are? Spider-Man? There's a big gap. You will fall and die."

"You're being dramatic," I respond. "I swing out to that tree and then wedge myself onto the windowsill and slide open the window and squish through. No big deal."

"Sounds insane," Hannah says. "You better let me go. I'm good at the monkey stuff. Remember I saved you on the *Nebula* when you were tangled in the netting ladder?"

The *Nebula* is a ship on which we were inadvertent stowaways and desperate to escape before we ended up in South America. And yes, I *remember* getting tangled up, even though I have tried hard to forget. "That was different," I say. "Seriously. You guys. I was a thief. Breaking and entering was part of the gig." They eyeball me, a united front, and I can tell what they are thinking. I was a *lousy* thief. I fell out of buildings. I got caught. My cheeks burn, and I glance down at my feet.

"We could send Zeus," Jin suggests.

"Send Zeus!" the bird hollers.

No way. What if he gets stuck? Or hurts himself? Or accidentally eats whatever is in that pail? "Forget it," I respond quickly. "Too risky."

"He can fly," Hannah reminds me. "I say we deploy the bird."

"He's not a missile!" I bark. "No. I'll go."

Unfortunately, our feathered pain in the butt does not agree with me on this particular matter. And before we can stop him, he takes off from his backpack perch and beelines right for the slim window opening.

CHAPTER 29

NOW HE'S GONE AND DONE IT

AT FIRST, I THINK ZEUS IS GOING TO CRASH INTO THE window at top speed, knock himself silly, and plunge to his death two stories below, the exact fate Jin predicted for me.

"Zeus!" I bellow, but he is already busy squeezing himself through the crack between the window and the sill.

Oh boy. I really wish he hadn't done that. We stand shoulder to shoulder, white-knuckling the railing, hearts racing. "Please don't get stuck," I whisper. "Please don't eat anything toxic."

Inside the apartment, Zeus does a lap and settles down right next to the pail. He pecks at it a few times, pulling something out with his beak.

"He's got this," Jin says with awe. "What a parrot!" But instead of returning to us, he suddenly flutters to the ceiling and disappears into the light fixture.

"What is he *doing*?" Hannah leans out over the railing as far as she can, scowling.

And that's when a woman enters the room. Her hair is all tucked up under a faded striped bucket hat, save a few silvery strands, and a bunch of bracelets run up her arm. Swiftly, she pulls down the poster of the symbol, rolls it tight, and tucks it under her arm. Scooping up the pail, she slides the white handle into the crook of her elbow. Next, she heads to the window and slams it shut.

No! No! No! She leaves the room without looking back.

As soon as the door closes, Zeus peeks out from his perch. Seeing the closed window, he hangs his head sadly. My heart snags. This is *not* good.

I'd like to say we remain calm and proceed in an orderly fashion. We don't. We panic.

Jin grabs my shoulders and gives me a shake. "Zeus is stuck in there!" he yells. As if I somehow missed it?

"I'm going after him," Hannah says, moving to climb over the railing.

"You are not!" I yell, pulling her back to the ground.

"We need to save Zeus!" she shouts.

We are making a lot of noise, and people stare. "Be quiet," I hiss. "*Think.*"

"I *am* thinking," Hannah growls. "Swing out to that tree. Wedge myself onto the windowsill. Break window. Squish through. Rescue bird. Find Midnight Market. Secure Helm. Hailed as heroes. Easy."

Jin gets a strange look on his face as he gazes at Hannah, something between shock and awe. "I never thought about the heroes part. That might be nice."

Hannah pokes him in the chest. "But *only* if we get the bird."

And Jin nods. "Get the bird," he repeats.

I see what is happening here. Hannah is brainwashing him so he agrees with her and it is two against one and I get outvoted and they execute Hannah's crazy plan and everything goes terribly and falls to pieces, and somehow we all end up in Judge Gold's courtroom and it is of course my fault. But I have no alternative to offer. And the truth is that I'm pretty sure Hannah can pull it off. She *is* better than me at the monkey stuff. There. I've said it.

Admitting this makes me feel a little like a deflated balloon. But sometimes being a good teammate means getting out of the way so someone else can shine. I take a deep breath, dig into my backpack, and pull out the

Window Witch 5.0. My friends look on with curiosity as I demonstrate.

"Super easy," I say. "So much better than 3.0. I mean, seriously. Not even the same at all." Why am I suddenly nervous? I know the original Window Witch worked, but what if this one is a complete fail? It hasn't exactly been field-tested. My mouth goes dry. My friends don't notice. Hannah snatches the Window Witch out of my hands.

"Gadgets," she says, examining it. "Excellent."

"Jin and I will run interference," I say. "Be fast."

She grins at me. "Is there any other way?" Her body quivers with excitement. Her eyes flash. "This is going to be *so* fun. I cannot *wait* to tell Bodhi."

The giant planters provide some protection from the eyes of tourists, but it is up to Jin and me to make sure they don't look too closely. Positioning ourselves to the side of the planters, I overturn my heavy backpack, sending its contents all over the walkway. "Oh shoot!" I shriek, dropping to my knees to collect my scattered belongings.

"This is terrible," Jin says loudly. With impressive dramatic flair, and seeing where I'm going with this, he attempts to help me. As long as my stuff obstructs the path, the stream of walkers moves off in the other direction, away from the apartment that Hannah is now illegally entering to save our wayward parrot. Rather than picking up all my bits of stuff, we spread them around and push them farther into the flow of people. It works like a dream. So maybe I'm not good at swinging from railings to trees to windows, but that's not everything.

From his position, Jin has eyes on Hannah. "She's in. She's got Zeus. She's back on the windowsill. Wow. She really is amazing, isn't she? I couldn't do that. Neither could you."

"Sure," I say through gritted teeth. "She's fabulous." I concentrate on collecting my things and stuffing them back in the pack while Jin provides a blow-by-blow of Hannah's safe and successful return to the High Line.

When she joins us on the pathway, she's exhilarated and hyper, hopping around like a lunatic. "That was amazing! Did you see me? I am *the best* at this stuff!" Zeus flutters from her shoulder to Jin and begins busily chewing his hair. I plan to have words with him later about obeying the commands of his human companions, as they are for his own good, but right now there is only one burning question that needs to be answered.

"Did you get it?" I ask, a little breathless.

Smiling slyly, Hannah opens her fist to reveal a small, round piece of metal, about the size of a quarter, nestled in her palm. "I had to pry it out of Zeus's mouth. He wanted to eat it."

Of course he did. I pluck it from her outstretched hand and examine the token's engraving. It's a majestic bird and a name. My friends huddle close. "What does it say?"

"The Phoenix Hotel," I reply.

"Where is that?" Hannah asks.

"Hey," Jin says. "Phoenix is the name of the treasure hunter who went rogue and vanished and terrible things happened to her and everything. Is this just a weirdo coincidence?"

A coincidence is when something unexpectedly happens at the same time or in the same way as something else. Whenever Dad encounters such a situation, he always gets a glint in his eye and says, "Well, look at *that* twist of fate." I never thought about it much until right now. Does he mean that coincidences are not as they seem but are *intentional*? Because fate does not feel random to me. It feels like destiny.

Thankfully, Hannah steps up to clarify. "So what?" she says. "There's a city named Phoenix in Arizona. And that kid in ninth grade at Redwood."

Jin grimaces. "Oh yeah. Him. I don't like him. He's kind of mean."

"Totally!" Hannah agrees, laughing. "He cheats at dodgeball! Who does that?"

They go back and forth like this, and while I think Hannah is probably right—it's simply a name, after all—I cannot rid myself of the tight, uncomfortable feeling lodged in my chest.

CHAPTER 30

GRAB-N-GO

FINDING THINGS WITHOUT A PHONE IS COMPLICATED. There are no phone booths anymore, so that means no phone books listing numbers and addresses of every location in the city. Instead, we pop into the chilly lobby of a towering sparkly hotel and tell the sympathetic concierge that we are lost. She agrees to call my dad, but then I realize I don't know his phone number. It's listed under "Dad" in my phone, and I never bothered to memorize it because . . . why? This worries the concierge a little too much. Quick on his feet, Jin reminds me that Dad said he'd meet us at the Phoenix Hotel. Right! The concierge provides the address, and we dash out of the hotel before she grows more suspicious.

The Phoenix Hotel turns out to be a forty-five-minute walk downtown, during which time the sun roasts us to a crisp. We complain bitterly, but the heat does not care and keeps gleefully beating down on us. Once we arrive at the address, it takes us a few extra minutes to actually find the entrance, which is tucked into a back alley barely visible from the street. The door is dingy red, but a gold medallion front and center bears the same phoenix symbol as the token.

"This must be it," I say, the little hairs on my arms standing at attention. It's creepy in this alley and much too quiet. If only the door had a window we could peer through to see what is on the other side. Hannah feels no such reservations. Hip-checking me out of the way, she shoves the door. Groaning on rusted hinges, it slowly swings inward, and a blast of musty air fragrant with garlic hits us hard. Jin sniffs, tilting his head to one side.

"Vampires," he says after a moment. "They must be using the garlic to ward them off."

"Or they're cooking," I reply. "Why does it have to be vampires?"

"Expect the unexpected." He disappears inside behind Hannah. I can't argue with that, so I brace for potential vampires and hotfoot it after my friends, anxious not to be left behind.

The hairs on my arms do not magically settle down once I'm inside. The air is thick and soupy. Shadows dance in the shafts of dim light penetrating the grimy windows. A thick layer of dust covers the heavy furniture and ornate reception desk, like no one has crossed the threshold in a very long time. An old fireplace mantel is laden with ceramic vases. Overflowing ashtrays are stacked on a side table beside a *Life* magazine from August 1952. A cocktail glass with a trace of ancient red lipstick rests on top of the magazine. The clutter reminds me a little of the inside of Great-Aunt Irma's San Francisco Victorian, minus the creepiness. I clutch the token in my hand like a talisman against whatever lurks in this hotel.

"Hello?" Hannah squeaks. Her voice ricochets around the gloomy lobby, but no one answers. We inch deeper into the space. Jin clutches my arm so hard he's going to leave a mark. But I get it. My heart pounds against my ribs. Zeus tucks his head under a feathery wing.

"Hello?" This time Hannah is louder, bolder. Still nothing. Maybe the garlic failed and everyone is sleeping in coffins down in the stony basement? That would be exciting and not in a good way. "There's no one here."

But a rustling behind a purple-and-yellow beaded curtain hanging in a door behind the reception desk suggests otherwise. "Who's there?" I ask. But there is no response.

"A cat?" Jin whispers, still holding on to me for dear life.

Suddenly, behind us a bright flash is followed by a blast of loud music. The room swirls with colored light, the kind a disco ball throws off. Do we all scream and jump a foot in the air? We might. You would too. This place is spooky. Against the far wall is a red carnival-game machine, one of those toy grabbers, pulsing with light and sound. *Grab-n-Go* is stenciled across its face in fancy gold script.

"What the heck?" Hannah says, trying to untangle herself from me and Jin. She approaches the Grab-n-Go, as if it might reach out and grab *her*. We move slowly in her wake, careful not to step on her heels.

Upon closer inspection, the Grab-n-Go is filled with stuffed animals and clear plastic balls containing trinkets like key chains and necklaces and cheap rings that turn your skin green. Thrown into the mix are several bright pink balls, smaller than the other ones and painted with the initials of the Midnight Market.

"We only have one token," Jin says, a little winded. "That means one try."

"Well, this is going to be an abrupt end to our journey," Hannah says flatly.

"Jin," I say. "You can totally do this. All those video games? It's the same thing. Focus. Concentration."

He looks at me, surprised. "Really? You think I can?"

"Absolutely," I reply. "No question." Although in reality I give it about a 65 percent chance of success. I fold the token into Jin's hand. "You got this."

Jin steps forward with a sharp look of concentration. "Just like a game," he mutters. "No big deal."

"Don't screw up," Hannah offers helpfully. I give her a swift kick in the shin. "Ouch!"

"Be quiet," I hiss.

"*Fine.*"

"Can the two of you please shut up?" Jin pleads. "Like, completely?" Taking a deep breath, he drops the token into the slot. The Grab-n-Go goes turbo, frantically flashing and belching bits of music into the dusty lobby. I take an involuntary step back. Jin grips the handle and begins to maneuver the claw into position over one of the balls. A digital reader counts down the seconds remaining in his turn. A bead of sweat forms on his upper lip. He lowers the claw, attempting to close it on the pink ball. But it slips from the claw's grasp and tumbles behind a small gray elephant with black eyes.

Jin wipes his damp forehead on the back of his sleeve.

He has thirty seconds left. My hands clench into tight fists. Clutching the handle, Jin raises the claw a second time and swings it over to another pink ball. I stop breathing. Hannah covers her face. The claw lowers, missing the ball and shoving it left, but Jin quickly adjusts and moves the claw back into position. Ten seconds. This is it. Now or never. The claw drops and its spiny metal fingers seize the pink ball fast.

With surgeonlike precision, Jin raises the claw, swings it over to the slot, and drops the pink ball inside. It clinks like chimes as it rolls out the chute and into his hand.

"You did it!" Hannah jumps up and down, clapping her hands.

Jin holds up the pink plastic ball, his face awash in the disco-ball colors. "I did, didn't I?" His pleased smile spreads wide, and his eyes get a little unfocused and dreamy.

"Made it look easy," I say. "Now open it."

"Right," he says, refocusing. "That was the whole point. Get the ball. See what's inside." Popping open the sphere, Jin pulls out a scrap of paper upon which a messy address is scratched in pen with the word "Congratulations!"

"Battery Park," Jin says, examining the slip.

"That's the very southern tip of Manhattan," Hannah says. "What else does it say?"

"Midnight. By the ferries."

We glance at one another. "I guess we know where we're going," I say. This should be exciting, but there is something about the flashing Grab-n-Go and the empty, dusty hotel lobby that tempers our enthusiasm. We have no idea what we are getting into.

Jin tosses the pink ball to Hannah and stuffs the paper into his pocket. "I'm not sure this is relevant, but I'm starving and we have no money." I'm about to suggest we get out of this place when the front door slams open and a hurricane of dust kicks up, blinding us.

Something is here.

CHAPTER 31

IT'S RAINING DRONES

THE AIR FILLS WITH THE BUZZ OF HELICOPTER ROTORS, and decades of dust fill my mouth. "A drone!" Jin shouts, shielding his head as the silver-winged quad races around the lobby, bumping into walls like it is short-circuiting. A mechanical arm on the underside of the drone clutches a thick padded envelope. The quad lurches in my direction. "Duck!" I hit the ground in time to save myself from a really bad haircut. Zeus zooms into the protective enclosure of the fireplace and huddles in the corner.

"What does it want?" Hannah yells. Oh, I don't know. To scare us witless? To kill us? To distract us? To ruin us? The possibilities are endless when you think about it.

I elbow-crawl toward a broom propped upright in the corner, intending to swat the quad out of the air, when it suddenly screeches to a halt and hovers above me, like an alien spaceship preparing to land on my head. But instead of landing, it drops the heavy padded envelope right at my feet and races out the door, knocking the old cocktail glass to the ground, where it shatters into a handful of tiny shards. In the aftermath, the place goes eerily quiet.

"Are we safe now?" Jin whispers.

"Are you kidding me with that question?" Hannah replies. "*Where* did it come from? *Why* was it here? *What* did it drop?"

Slowly, I pull the heavy envelope toward me. *Treasure Hunters* is scrawled across the front in black marker. Hannah crawls on hands and knees and plops down beside me. "That's us," she says definitively. "Hunters."

"Open it," Jin urges. But he cringes back as if he expects the package to explode. This might be worse than vampires. I slide a tentative finger under the flap, but I don't get far.

"Time to go," Zeus suddenly squawks, flapping around in my face so I can't ignore him.

"Stop that!"

"*Now!*" Zeus insists.

"Um . . . Lola?" Jin nudges me, and I follow his gaze. Behind the curtain, a pair of yellow eyes gleam in the darkness. Cat eyes. But it must be a big cat. A really *big* cat.

"Now! Now! Now!" Zeus explodes in a burst of feathery impatience.

"Got it," I whisper. "Going. Right now." I grab the envelope, and we back cautiously out of the Phoenix Hotel. Well, not Zeus. He flies as fast as he can.

The light outside is somehow brighter and sharper than when we went in. Squinting, we run down the alley away from the gritty red door until there is a comfortable distance between us and it. Leaning against a building wall, we stop to catch our breath.

"What is a mountain lion doing in New York?" Jin asks, wheezing.

"There was a guy here once who kept a Bengal tiger named Ming in his apartment," I reply, wiping sweat from my forehead. "He didn't get caught until Ming mauled him and he ended up in the hospital." Jin and Hannah both stare at me. "I swear. It's true. What?"

"What *happened*?" Jin cries.

"To the guy? He was fine."

"No! To the tiger!"

"Oh. He went to a zoo in Ohio. The guy also had an

alligator named Al in the apartment. I don't know what happened to him." Strange things happen in New York City. Seriously. "I think this envelope is full of rocks."

But tucked inside are three yellow-and-blue subway passes, fifteen crisp ten-dollar bills, and a gold bar about the size of a pack of playing cards, engraved with an intricate phoenix, much like the token but more complex, including snakes intertwined with flowers along the bottom. Sparkling in the evening sun, it looks like it belongs in a museum, so beautiful it's a little mesmerizing. Jin snatches the gold bar from my hands.

"Hey!"

"Is it like a gold doubloon?" he asks, peering at it from different angles.

"Yes," says Hannah snidely. "Because coins are often rectangular."

"No need to be snotty," Jin says with a sniff. "Clearly the subway passes are for transportation and the money is for food, so what is the gold bar that is not a doubloon for?"

"To trade for the Helm?" I suggest. Because honestly, no one is going to give us the Helm in exchange for Ping-Pong smoke bombs or a lavender-infused bandanna.

But who exactly sent it? Lipstick? My dad? Our fairy godmother? Oh right. We don't have one of those. Lipstick?

This is the perfect opportunity for me to explain my late-night conversation, but Hannah pipes up about not being able to figure anything out until she eats, and Jin, in complete agreement, jumps in to suggest cheeseburgers, fries, and milkshakes from that little place around the bend from the alley. And another opportunity slips by.

When our last slurp of milkshake is gone, we head downtown to Battery Park, compliments of our subway passes. Figuring out how to ride the subway is no easy thing when you are a newbie. At one point I think we are headed somewhere totally off the wall like *Staten Island*, but finally we arrive at our intended destination.

Battery Park is located on the southern tip of Manhattan Island. Ferries depart here to the Statue of Liberty as well as a number of other places. We have time to kill, so we wander over to the SeaGlass Carousel, housed in an enormous steel-and-glass building the shape of a nautilus. Although the carousel is closed to riders, thirty giant fish, illuminated by ever-changing lights, glow in the night. It is like something out of a very weird dream.

"It looks like the bioluminescence from the ocean," Hannah says. "Like the light thrown off from living creatures."

"It's cool," Jin says, tilting his head for a different view.

We stand there for a long time, gazing at the huge sparkly fish and thinking our own thoughts. Finally, we leave the carousel and move on, passing a memorial to victims of the Irish Potato Famine and Merchant Mariners' Memorial, right at the water's edge. That one makes my mouth dry. There are three bronze sailors on a boat, one reaching for a fourth, who is overboard and busy drowning. I hope this is not a premonition or a sign or whatever.

Jin reads the plaque. "Check it out," he says, pointing at the sailors. "At high tide the drowning guy vanishes, and at low tide you can see him."

Hannah sighs. "He's always in some state of drowning. Forever. For all eternity. It's a drag."

"He's made of bronze," Jin reminds her.

"Still," she replies.

I glance at my watch. Eleven thirty. Time to focus. Instead of being tucked in our beds, fast asleep, we occupy a bench with a clear view of the ferry terminals, on the lookout for anything unusual. The park is pushed up against the Hudson River, and the water is dark and ominous, covered by a low-hanging mist. There are a surprising number of people milling around, considering how late it is. A group with small dogs congregates about twenty feet away, and another with shopping bags. There's a lady with a stroller who looks tired and grumpy, and a young guy, headphones on, juggling a bunch of balls. I guess they don't call it the City That Never Sleeps for nothing. Or maybe it's just too hot to sleep.

The clock ticks slowly forward. I try not to check my watch every second, but the thing is obviously broken because time is barely moving at all. One of Dad's favorite sayings is "A watched pot never boils." It annoys me. I mean, does staring at water have any impact on the physics of it boiling? No, it doesn't. It's *science*. It just *is*, whether you believe it or not. I glance at my watch again and growl.

"Are you guys tired?" Jin asks.

"No," Hannah says quickly, eyes scanning the water like she is some sort of robot. "Are you?"

Stifling a yawn, Jin replies, "No way. I'm good. Totally awake. Ready for anything. What about you, Lola?"

I wouldn't describe what I'm feeling as tired exactly. It's more complicated, a mix of dread and anticipation with a dash of fear that makes my stomach gurgle. But I don't want to say this to my friends. I want them to think my nerves are steady and calm, even if this is not entirely true. "I'm good. Not tired. Completely awake." I glance at my watch. Midnight.

"I wish something would *happen*," Hannah complains.

And in that moment, as if conjured by Hannah, a barge appears out of the mist, like a big metal ghost plowing silently through the water. When it is still about forty feet from the river's edge, it suddenly explodes with light. Twinkle lights and flashing lights and spotlights, bright as stars. Mounted on the cabin is a spinning disc, about five feet in diameter, comprised of flaming sparklers in red and green. It's the *MM* symbol, hissing and spitting and billowing smoke into the night air.

"What the *heck*?" Jin shields his eyes. The lights dim just as quickly as the barge glides alongside the retaining wall. A ramp extends to land. Stroller Lady efficiently folds up the stroller like an umbrella and marches toward the ramp. Headphones Guy stops his exercise and he, too, heads for the barge. One of the dog people tucks his pint-size fur baby under his arm and joins the parade of about twenty random people.

"This is so *it*!" Hannah says, leaping to her feet. "Let's go!" She charges toward the ramp. We run after her. I clutch the gold bar to keep it from bouncing out of my pocket.

"Is this a good idea?" Jin asks, his voice shaky.

No. Definitely not. But it never is, and we end up doing it anyway. "It will be fine," I say. Oddly, my fear and dread are gone, replaced by excitement about what is going to happen next. This is good. Fear is not wrong or bad, but it can get out of control and in the way.

As soon as my feet hit the ramp, I have a spasm of panic. What if they ask for a ticket? What if they say there's an age limit? Or a height limit? Or they don't want us here?

Chill out, Lola. Stay cool and get on like everyone else is.

We queue up behind the others. I wonder if Lipstick's nemesis is here and if we will have to wrestle her for the Helm. A surge of guilt rises up. How would I explain that to my friends exactly? It's completely silent as everyone shuffles forward at the same slow pace. Even the sounds of the city—honking horns, sirens, shouting—seem muffled. At the end of the ramp is a young man in a crisp white uniform, a sparkly badge of the *MM* symbol fixed to his jacket. Silently, he holds out a silver bowl. As passengers board, they silently place the small pink balls, just like the one we got from the Grab-n-Go, into a silver bowl, where they jingle like bells. Hannah extracts ours from her pocket and tosses it in, and just like that, we are *on* the barge.

"You know," Jin whispers, "if we fall overboard and drown, there will be no record of us having been here. It will be like those scuba divers that got left behind at the Great Barrier Reef in Australia because the captain didn't take attendance before going back to land. They got eaten by sharks. Just FYI."

"I don't think this river is infested with sharks," I whisper back.

"It has to connect to the ocean *somewhere*," Jin points out. Currently, sharks are very low down on my list of concerns. I hold a finger to my lips to silence him. I'd hate to get kicked off the barge because we have somehow broken the golden rule of no talking.

As soon as everyone is on board, the ramp rolls up and the barge lurches away from shore. No turning back now.

CHAPTER 32

THE MIDNIGHT MARKET

IN THE DARKNESS, THE PASSENGERS SEEM LIKE GHOSTS, with blurry edges, blending into one another. There are many more people on board than who got on with us. Maybe the barge makes stops, like a bus? I jump when Hannah appears beside me, grabbing my hand.

"This is trippy," she says, cheeks flushed.

"I *know* they have lights," Jin complains. "Why not turn them on?"

"Stealth mode," I say. The barge deck is wide and crowded, and the stink of smoke from the sparklers lingers. "We should split up. Check things out. Report back."

"Please remember the last time we were on a boat

together, we had to jump for our lives," Jin says gravely. "Let's try not to do that again. Okay?" We agree, and Jin and Hannah head in opposite directions while I cut down the middle. For a supposed market, there does not look like anything is for sale. There are no tables or display cases or anything. It's possible we just got on a random barge for a midnight river tour. That would be funny but also bad.

When I can get a look at the passengers' faces, their expressions are all the same. Serene, patient, relaxed, as if they have done this before. But maybe if you deal in magical mythical potentially dangerous treasures, nothing is surprising anymore?

I weave through the ethereal people. Some are young, maybe a few years older than us, and others are quite elderly and wrinkled. No one has their face buried in a smartphone. In fact, I don't see a single glowing rectangle. Maybe it's frowned upon? Or illegal even? But I get the sense the whole market is illegal, so would people willing to break rules be worrying about them? Whatever the reason, heads are up and the passengers are quietly watching the dark world of water whiz by.

Wind in my face indicates that we are moving down the river at a good clip, slipping between the round end of Brooklyn and Staten Island, leaving the city lights behind us. Chop on the water sends the barge surfing up and down the waves. We are out in open ocean. Are barges meant for seafaring? I thought they hauled garbage around and stuff. I'm holding on to the rail to steady myself when a boy about my age staggers up next to me, his face an unnatural shade of green.

"Watch out," he groans. "Gotta puke." Gross! I jump to one side as the boy barfs over the edge. "Oh. That's the worst. Uh-oh. More." I close my eyes and wait for the retching sounds to subside. When I open them, the boy is slumped over the railing, about to pitch headfirst into the water. Did he pass out? Instinctively, I grab the back of his shirt and haul him back onto the deck. He collapses in a heap at my feet, where I nudge him with a toe to make sure he's breathing. After a moment, he wipes his mouth on the bottom hem of his T-shirt, leaving a brown smear right through the words *Chappaqua Country Day*, written in bright red.

Chappaqua Country Day? I know that school. *Why* do I know that school? My brain lurches around, looking for the connection. "Is that your school?" I ask, gesturing at the shirt.

The boy glances down as if he forgot what he was wearing. "What? Oh. Yeah."

But before I can ask for details, the boat lurches and I step right on the boy's knee. "Ow!"

"Sorry!" I offer him a hand up. He dusts himself off, except he can't do much with the smear on his T-shirt.

"You should know that I wasn't really going to fall overboard," he says, eyeing me. "I had it under control. Like, totally."

You totally didn't, but if that idea embarrasses you, then fine, I think to myself. I smile benignly. Another boy, a carbon copy of Barf Boy in the same school T-shirt, appears out of the gloom.

"Dude," he says. "We thought you bought it."

Barf Boy punches his friend in the biceps, hard. The friend winces. "I'm fine," Barf Boy says. "Let's go." He does not even glance at me as he disappears into the crowd. Well, that wasn't very polite. I saved his life, after all. This is what I'm thinking when the barge suddenly slows and explodes once again with light.

It is utterly *transformed.* Flickering candles are strung above our heads, and glass crystals drip like raindrops alongside them. Mirrors line the wheelhouse and reflect the kaleidoscope of colors thrown off by an old-school disco ball dangling from the masthead light. Music blasts from unseen speakers. Waiters dressed in smart black-and-white uniforms move among the guests with trays of food and frosty drinks. Some passengers throw off layers, revealing party outfits that glitter and shimmer as much as the barge herself does. A woman with silver hair, dressed in a sequined jumpsuit, with what must be a thousand strands of glittering beads around her neck, jumps up on an overturned packing crate, microphone clutched in her hand. She sparkles so brightly, it's like looking directly into the sun.

"My lovelies!" Sparkle Lady bellows. "Welcome to the Midnight Market! And, more importantly, welcome to international waters, where the only law is . . . there is no law!" Everyone cheers. Some people jump up and down and clap their hands like Santa Claus just popped out of the chimney. "And remember, folks, what happens in international waters *stays* in international waters." A roar of laughter rises from the crowd. It's clear they love her, hanging on her every word. "Oh, how I've missed you! I could stand up here all night and catch up, but I won't. We have curated an extraordinary collection of items for you this year, and I know you are anxious to see them. Remember you can beg, barter, or buy, but that is between you and the seller."

While she's talking, another barge of about the same

size appears out of the shadows and maneuvers into position beside us. "And as you can see, we are ready to receive you. Happy shopping, my people." At the wave of her hand, the new barge extends a gangplank linking the two boats together. The *second* barge is the actual market.

Suddenly beside me, Jin whispers, "This is kind of overwhelming." He twists his Paul bracelet frantically.

"Yeah," I agree. I didn't know what to expect, but I know it wasn't this.

Hannah emerges from the crowd. "This is wild," she says breathlessly. "What is the word when something is so beyond amazing that it might actually break the space-time continuum and change life as we know it forever?"

"Really cool?" Jin suggests.

Hannah rolls her eyes. "Thanks. Brilliant. And why are you guys just standing here? Let's get the Helm!" She yanks us toward the people queuing to board the second barge.

As we shove our way into the line, I notice Barf Boy a few yards away. I also notice Jin notice Barf Boy. And when he does, all the color drains from his face.

CHAPTER 33

SHOP LIKE YOU MEAN IT

THE SECOND BARGE IS MORE LIKE AN UPSCALE FLEA market, very orderly in contrast to the three-ring circus currently raging on the other boat, if you don't count the inflatable lifeboats, big bundles of black rubber stowed along the railings. It's *a lot* of lifeboats. I mean, safety first and all, but what do they think is going to happen? There are a number of burly security guards circulating on deck.

As we step off the gangway, a man in a tuxedo reminds us to mind our manners. "Violence will get you thrown overboard," he states as if he is a flight attendant instructing the passengers on how to buckle their seat belts. "And no rescue will be provided."

Got it. Don't act like a bully or a jerk. Behave. If not, prepare to swim. When I turn to Jin to make a joke about us always ending up in the water, one way or another, he's gone.

"Hey." I nudge Hannah. "Where is Jin?" Hannah, laser-focused on the task at hand, does not know or particularly care.

"He's here somewhere," she mutters. "Hard to get lost on a boat." Tables fill every inch of space on the barge deck. As we weave in and out, searching, we see some very interesting things. A jar of iridescent slimy worms that, when eaten, enable a person to understand any language or form of communication for twenty-four hours. But do not eat them and drink soda at the same time because you might explode.

There are rows of exquisite-looking chocolate bonbons that will turn you into a temporary genius. But if you eat more than one at a time, your brain may heat up and fry. There is Cinderella's glass slipper on a purple pillow with yellow tassels. No really. I swear. We stop briefly to examine a table of breathtakingly beautiful walnut-size glass balls filled with oozy, glowing glitter. The seller grins, exposing a mouth of rotten teeth.

"Nice, eh?" she says. Her eyes are milky and clouded, and I get the weird sensation that she can see right into my brain. "Princess crystals. In the minor-magic category but still very useful. They won't make you invisible or let you fly or get you endless future wishes or shower you in gold coins. Not the sort of thing you might use to take over the world, you know . . ." At this point she stops to laugh at her own joke, which I have to say I do not find funny at all, considering the circumstances. "But if you need a little nudge of magic, if you have a simple wish that needs answering, princess crystals come highly recommended. Choosing wisely is the key. Not all crystals like all people."

Great. Cranky crystal balls. "No thanks," I say politely. "We are looking for something else."

"We are *all* searching all the time," the seller says with a wink.

Huh? I barely have time to process her meaning before Hannah gives me a shove. "Let's *go*!" There will be no browsing magical mythical potentially dangerous treasures today.

We rush past a table of enchanted Instant Pots. The sign reads:

WILL COOK ANYTHING YOUR HEART DESIRES IN AN INSTANT!

WARNING: MAY SPONTANEOUSLY COMBUST

There are strings of effervescent necklace beads designed to make you feel bubbly; gurgling purple potions to jinx your enemies; spells and hexes, scribbled on parchment, to further your most nefarious objective. There are flying bird feathers with sharpened poisoned points and frogs that, if you kiss them, do not turn into princes but instead cover your body with warts. Are people really dumb enough to fall for that?

There are stockpot-size cast-iron cauldrons, claiming to perform modern alchemy on your stove top. Add a few shakes of special salt, a base metal, and some water. Boil for ten minutes and, boom, gold coins!

A row of aromatic candles turn introverts into extroverts. PERFECT FOR THAT PARTY YOU REALLY DON'T WANT TO GO TO BUT HAVE TO ANYWAY, claims the sign. The next table sports a collection of handheld mirrors, bedazzled with rhinestones, promising fifty minutes of exquisite inner and outer beauty. The small print warns that the mirrors' definition of inner and outer beauty may not align with that of the person gazing upon it. Well, that is reassuring.

There is even a seller who claims to have the Honjo Masamune, a legendary samurai sword that went missing from Japan during World War II, but I can tell, even from a distance, that it's fake. I'm not famous archaeologist Lawrence Benko's daughter for nothing.

"Hey, Lola?"

"Hey, Hannah?" I reply, my gaze still on the sword.

"*There.*" Hannah points to a table piled high with cheap baseball hats, embroidered with ordinary team logos, all slightly off. But nestled in with the hats is a gleaming golden crown, heavy with jewels and stamped with an ivy pattern. The Helm is a *crown*? Well, sure it is. Back in the olden times of mythology, people wore crowns. It was no big thing.

Behind the table is a bedraggled older man in a tattered safari vest who looks like he could use a good meal and a nap. His mustache aspires to be handlebar, but the damp air has left it limp. Straggly ends hang down below his chin, making him the spitting image of a walrus.

"Interested in hats?" he asks, bushy eyebrows twitching. "Well, I have the most important hats, hats that do something very mind-blowing. Something life-changing. Something *epic*. Do you want to know what that is?"

We nod, a captive audience of two, waiting for his words of wisdom.

"They protect your nose from sunburn!" He laughs, slapping his knee. "And your scalp. Very important. Sunburn is no joke."

"Very funny," Hannah says, planting her feet. "But we

are interested in that." She points at the crown. "It's the Helm of Darkness. Right?"

Walrus takes a step back. "Slow down there, little lady. You are talking a big game here, definitely driving outside your lane. Might I suggest you kids run along and buy some princess rocks? They are more your speed." He gestures toward the princess crystals.

"We don't do rocks," I say bluntly. "Not anymore."

"Yeah," agrees Hannah. "Been there. Done that."

"We are shopping for the Helm," I say.

"You can't *afford* the Helm," Walrus says with an exasperated sigh. "It's worth more than your two puny lives put together."

Boy, he really woke up on the wrong side of the bed this morning. Is it because we didn't laugh at his sunburn joke? "You should know our lives are actually worth quite a lot," Hannah replies.

"Fine, then," Walrus scoffs. "Show me what you've got to trade that is *so* valuable."

Hannah turns to me. "Show him." She means the gold bar, but I'm suddenly not keen to part with it. It's so pretty and, I don't know, heavy. Maybe there is something else Walrus will accept? I reach deep into my backpack and pull out the Ping-Pong balls.

"Smoke bombs?" I ask.

"Are you kidding me?" Walrus replies. I guess not.

"How about a lavender-infused bandanna with a built-in fan?" I suggest.

"To help me relax?" he asks, glaring at me.

"You could use a little relaxing," I say. "If we're being honest."

"Okay. Enough. Time to move along, you aggravating youngsters. I have real customers waiting." I stuff the bandanna in my pocket.

"The gold *bar*, Lola," Hannah hisses.

Walrus's ears perk right up at that. "A gold bar, you say?"

Slowly, I extract the bar from my pocket and hold it up. It glows brightly, as if lit from within. By comparison, the crown is shabby. As I turn the bar in my hands, Walrus's eyes latch on to it, but in a flash his expression goes slack.

"Could it *be*?" he breathes. "Is it real?" Leaping from behind his table, he snatches the bar from my outstretched hands before I have time to react.

"Hey!" I protest.

But he doesn't hear me as he turns the gold bar greedily over in his hands. His mustache trembles. "It really *is*. A Phoenix bar. In the possession of a couple of kids. *Where* did you get this? Tell me at once."

"We have our sources," Hannah says quickly because really we have no idea. "Now give it back or give us the Helm."

"Yes! Yes! Of course!" Walrus falls all over himself agreeing. "You have a deal. Absolutely. Take the Helm. Please."

Wait! No! I mean, we came here for the Helm, but part of me feels like we are making a big mistake. It's that word again. Phoenix. I'm starting to lean toward twist of fate rather than coincidence. Everything is moving too fast! My eyebrow spasms.

Come on, Lola! Get it together! What is wrong with you?

Whoever delivered the gold bar meant for us to use it in this way. It means nothing while the Helm means *everything.*

But the Walrus doesn't box up the crown and hand it over. Instead, he pats down the many pockets of his vest and eventually pulls out a baseball cap, crushed almost beyond recognition. He gives it a few good shakes, and the cap straightens out. Instead of a team logo front and center, the cap has flames, and I *swear* I see them flicker. The Walrus holds out the hat.

"The Helm of Darkness," he says with no ceremony.

"No way," replies Hannah. "What about this?" She gestures at the crown.

"Paperweight," he says with a shrug. "Literally. It keeps

my invoices from blowing away while we're on this boat. You can have it if you want, but it is worthless."

"Prove it," I say. My unease grows. I do not want to leave here swindled. I don't think my ego could take another setback.

"Kids," Walrus says with a sigh. "So annoying." He does a once-over of all those pockets again, removing a phone, a watch, and a set of headphones. "FYI, the hat will fry your electronics. Learned that lesson the hard way." Satisfied, he gently places the cap on his matted thatch of hair.

And Walrus *disappears*.

"Oh. Wow." Hannah and I lean into each other.

"He's *gone*," I whisper.

"It really *is* the Helm."

"We found it."

"Of course we did," Hannah whispers. "You didn't doubt us, did you?"

Well, maybe a little. Once or twice. Walrus's disembodied voice floats out from empty space. "If you wear the cap and touch another person, they, too, will become invisible." Suddenly, Hannah vanishes. I yelp in surprise, knocking Walrus's water bottle into the air. When the spilled water hits him, I can see the faintest shimmering outline of his arm.

"Hannah!"

She giggles. "I'm right here." I can feel her fingers tickle my face, but I can't see them. It takes weird to a whole new level. Walrus pulls off the cap, and he and Hannah reappear. Hannah shakes herself out like a wet dog. "So *strange*. Like being walked all over by a million tiny kitten paws."

"You probably get used to it if you wear the cap enough," Walrus says. "Are you satisfied?" He clutches the gold bar in such a way that I think even if we decide not to take the Helm, we won't get the bar back.

"Yes," I say finally. "Done deal." And I take the Helm of Darkness from Walrus's gnarled hand.

CHAPTER 34

NOW IT'S A PARTY!

I'D LIKE TO SAY THAT IN THE NEXT MOMENT WE celebrate our victory by taking turns donning the Helm and vanishing, just for kicks. But no. That would be too simple, and one thing I have learned is that hunting for magical mythical potentially dangerous treasures is *never* simple.

Because before we can revel in our success, before Hannah can explain about the kitten paws, a blaring siren shatters the night, causing me to nearly jump out of my skin. Everyone on board the second barge freezes in place. An announcement crackles over the PA system. It's Sparkle Lady. "Sorry, folks. Party's over. Our *friends* are incoming. Three minutes to disembark."

Huh? I glance at Hannah, who shakes her head. She's clueless too. But our fellow passengers know the drill. Without missing a beat, the sellers swiftly pack up their wares, while the buyers begin to throw the lifeboats overboard. As soon as the black bundles hit the water, they pop and fizz like shaken cans of soda and explode outward, quickly taking shape.

"Abandon ship!" Sparkle Lady shouts gleefully. No one panics. I think they are actually having fun. Black boats fill the water, barely visible. Passengers climb up onto the railings and leap into them with hoots of laughter.

I clutch the Helm to my chest. *Where* is Jin? The barge is in full-chaos mode now, with people throwing themselves overboard with wild abandon. More boats pop and fizz until the ocean is awash with them.

And that's when a police boat, lights flashing, emerges from the fog. Oh, so *that's* the problem. "We need to get out of here," I say. "Like, *now*. Where is Jin?"

"I don't know!" Hannah yells. In the darkness, it's impossible to see who is who. "He probably got off already. Let's *go*!"

Would Jin do that, jump off without us? My instincts say no, but as the police boat closes in, we are left with little choice. Hannah charges for the railing. But when I attempt to follow, something holds me fast. Or *someone.* It's Sparkle Lady, grinning in a way that seems totally out of place, considering the circumstances.

"Here," she says. "Take these. They come in handy at the strangest moments." She presses a pair of princess crystals into my hands, but she doesn't let go. She gazes at me. "You look so much like her, it really is *remarkable.*"

What? *Who* do I look like? Behind me, Hannah bellows for me to hurry up. And in that split second when I'm distracted, Sparkle Lady folds into the fray and I hear a musical note, like tinkling bells, or shattering glass or crystal butterfly wings. Her *necklaces.*

"Lola! *Now!*" The urgency in Hannah's voice snaps me back to the rather critical present. Midnight Market. Police. Escape. *Got it.*

"I'm coming!" I yell, shoving the princess crystals deep in my pocket.

Hannah and I scale the railing and, holding hands, hurl ourselves into the closest floaty boat. But a wave rolls in and tosses the stern of the lightweight vessel up in the air. Which means I land in the ocean.

At least the Atlantic Ocean in summer is fairly pleasant, even if it does feel like I'm on the spin cycle in a washing machine. A wave crashes over my head. I hang on to the Helm for dear life, my backpack suddenly an anchor pulling me down.

"Lola!" Hannah holds out her hand, and I lunge for it but come up short. Treading frantically, I pull the lavender bandanna from my pocket and wave it toward her to extend my reach. But it is not enough, and her boat drifts away, leaving me swirling in the murky waves.

I can't give up, however I'm seriously considering it, when there is a voice behind me. "Hang on!" Water fills my mouth when I try to answer, but I wave the bandanna overhead like an SOS flag. I'm here!

Two boats bear down on my location. In seconds, one of the boats is practically on my head, but I can't get a grip on the slippery rubber side and rescue myself. We *do* always end up in the water. Why is that?

Hey, Lola! Save that mystery until you are not actively drowning! Jeez!

Right. First things first. Sandwiched between the two rubber boats, I hold up the bandanna and someone grabs it, yanking me close enough that I can get ahold of a tether clipped to the end of the raft. With no grace, I heave myself directly into an empty boat, where I sprawl across the bottom, gasping for air. "Thank you," I mutter, getting to my hands and knees. Water streams from my hair. I experience a wave of nausea that I attribute to drinking a Big Gulp of salt water.

My rescuer, drifting away in the second boat, replies, "You are *so* welcome." This is followed by laughter, the kind that makes the little hairs on my arms stand up. I squint to get a better look at who it is and catch a flash of . . . something? But another wave broadsides the boat, and I grab the handle with an empty hand just before pitching overboard.

My *empty* hand. The Helm is *gone*.

"No! No! No!" I drop back to my knees and frantically search the bottom of the boat. I know I had it! And there is no way I dropped it. "This cannot be happening," I groan. When I glance up, the perfectly camouflaged boats have dispersed, dozens of them traveling in different directions, like a herd of spooked sheep. It's virtually impossible for the police to see them or round them up. It's a brilliant escape plan. If I weren't in the armpit of complete despair, I'd take a moment to admire its simplicity. My little boat is equipped with a silent electric motor that automatically propels me toward a distant shore.

I'm completely alone. No friends. No Helm. They even stole my lavender-infused bandanna with the built-in fan! Who *does* that? And everything had gone so well! Of course, that is the first sign that you are headed for disaster. I tuck myself against the side of the boat and bury my head in my knees.

I'm about to cry. Seriously. I normally save crying for extreme circumstances, but an inventory of what just happened proves this might qualify. Tears brim at the corners of my eyes when Zeus swoops out of the darkness and perches on my shoulder, like nothing eventful has happened. I'm so happy to see him that the tears spill over. This is pushing the boundaries of what is acceptable behavior in a crisis.

"Zeus!" He nestles into my neck and coos. I stroke his damp feathers. "Where's Jin? Where's Hannah? Are you okay? Where am *I*?"

"Lola." Zeus sounds serious, as if he is about to deliver grave information. "Dinner, Lola."

He digs his claws into my shoulder to make sure I understand.

"Quit that," I say. "I'll get you something to eat when we land." Whenever and wherever that is. The little boat moves along at a good clip, slicing through the water. The city lights come into focus. We are back in the mouth of the river. The fog dissipates. My eyes are still hazy from salt water, but ahead of me are a dozen other black lifeboats, all heading in different directions, rendering the police effort completely pointless. It really *is* a brilliant escape plan.

In the distance, the Statue of Liberty looms. She looks disappointed in me. Great. Fifteen minutes later, my boat glides to a pier at Ellis Island, the world's busiest immigration port until the 1950s, and now one of the biggest tourist attractions along with the Statue of Liberty. The dock is designed for ferryboats, which makes climbing out no joke. As soon as my feet are clear, the little boat navigates back into the river, vanishing in the night.

Oh, I am going to be in such trouble when they find me in the morning. My friends are missing. The Helm is gone, and I'm stranded in the middle of New York Harbor. I lie on the grass and stare up at the night sky while Zeus hops around, nudging me, as if he's worried I've gone and died before fetching him the promised meal. Struggling, I get to my feet. And that's when Hannah charges me.

"Oh my God!" she wails. "I thought you drowned!" She hugs me hard. But quickly pushes me away. "Do you have it? Where is it?"

I shake my head, the tears welling up once again. "I don't know what happened," I cry. "I had it in my hand. And then I got pulled onto a boat. And then I don't know . . ."

"You guys!" It's the missing Jin, dripping wet and headed our way. I'm relieved he's okay, but I'm also furious.

"Where did you *go*?" I demand. "I had the Helm!"

"Until she lost the Helm," Hannah adds. I want to kick her, but she's exactly right. It takes us a moment to realize Jin's eyes are pinwheeling in his head and his face is the color of shock, which in Jin's case is vampire pale, just FYI.

"Wait. Are you okay?" I ask. "Was it the near drowning? Did Zeus say something mean? He can do that, you know."

Jin waves his hands to cut me off. "No." Distress is evident on his face. Whatever happened, he feels it deep in his guts. "I did something. I didn't mean to. Or actually, I did, but I shouldn't have. And now I don't know what to do. I don't know how to fix it."

Warm water breaks loose in my ear canal and trickles out onto my shoulder. But it must free up some space in there for connections because a few things come together in that lightning-fast way that doesn't make any sense later on.

And it all centers on those Chappaqua T-shirts.

CHAPTER 35

STAR AND FISH SCREW IT ALL UP

STAR: *Where on earth are you? The last thing I saw was you jumping into one of those getaway boats!*

FISH: *Unsure. But from the looks of it, maybe Staten Island?*

STAR: *I thought you were dead.*

FISH: *Did you find that upsetting?*

STAR: *Jury is still out.*

FISH: *Gee, thanks.*

STAR: *What are you doing on Staten Island?*

FISH: *I thought I saw the Helm. There was a guy with a golden crown tucked under his arm, so I jumped into his getaway boat. It wasn't the Helm. It was a paperweight. The guy laughed, told me to go learn my history, and pushed me overboard. It was insulting. And now I'm stuck on Staten Island.*

STAR: *Did you swim there?*

FISH: *No! I got picked up by another boat, but they didn't believe I had any authority to arrest them for trafficking in magical objects. They laughed at me too, but at least they didn't pitch me over the side. It's not been a great day.*

STAR: *For the record, I would like to say I did not agree to this plan at the start. I take no responsibility at all for the outcome.*

FISH: *What are you talking about? This whole plan was your idea!*

STAR: *It was certainly not!*

FISH: *You were the one who would not stop complaining about Siberia. The only reason we are here is because you wanted to go surfing. Thus, this is all your fault.*

STAR: *I cannot believe you.*

FISH: *And I cannot believe I let you talk me into using a police boat to break up the Midnight Market after what happened the last time we used a police boat to raid the Midnight Market.*

STAR: *Are you referring to the situation in the Son Doong Cave in Vietnam? It's the biggest cave in the world! It has a river and a jungle and could easily fit an entire small city inside it. That was so not our fault.*

FISH: *It was kind of our fault. Mostly yours. Like it is now.*

STAR: *It's not fair that all our bad ideas end up being my ideas.*

FISH: *Well, there is a big difference between my ideas and your ideas. My ideas work and yours fail. Every. Single. Time. And I have data to support my argument. Unfortunately.*

STAR: *Whatever. Now you're being mean about it.*

FISH: *Anyway, I'd love to debate this for the next one hundred years, but we have real problems to solve and they are fairly urgent. We lost the Helm—that's what we should be focused on. Those Midnight Marketers are the worst.*

STAR: *You have to admit, it was a pretty good getaway plan.*

FISH: *No, I do not, and no, it wasn't! It was a terrible idea.*

STAR: *Only because it worked.*

FISH: *I hate them.*

STAR: *What do we do now? Can Moose rescue you?*

FISH: *He's still AWOL. I'm starting to get suspicious.*

STAR: *Is it time to panic?*

FISH: *What? No! We regroup. We wait. We exercise patience. We make up a really good story to tell the bosses.*

STAR: *Wonderful. I'm going out for a latte. Good luck getting off that island.*

FISH: *You are a bad partner.*

CHAPTER 36

WHAT JIN DID

HANNAH SITS DOWN ON A BENCH, THE STATUE OF Liberty blinking in the distance. "I guess you better tell us," she says. I wedge in next to her.

Jin paces in a tight circle, gathering his thoughts, occasionally glancing up at Lady Liberty as if to gather strength. Twice he tries to speak but nothing comes out, just a few tiny squeaks. He's in a bad way.

"It's Chappaqua, isn't it?" I say finally. Jin stops abruptly. Does he look relieved or terrified? I can't tell. Barf Boy had on a gray Chappaqua Country Day T-shirt. Chappaqua Country Day is the school where *Paul* goes. And to make matters worse, I now realize the kid who saved me from drowning, who stole the Helm, was also wearing a Chappaqua Country Day shirt. "Paul was on the barge. And his friends. You told him everything about treasure hunting, didn't you?"

Jin's face crumples, and that is how I know I'm right.

Hannah leaps to her feet. "What do you *mean* Paul was on the boat?" she shouts. "*Paul* Paul?"

"I told him about the Midnight Market before we left camp," Jin says forlornly. "He said it sounded so excellent and he wished he could go."

"But how did he know where we were going when we didn't even know where we were going?" Hannah shouts again. "You better not have that stupid phone in your shoe."

Jin throws his arms up in the air. "I said I didn't have it!" But that's when I notice the bracelet, the *Paul* bracelet, and the microchip charm.

"The bracelet," I say. "He's *tracking* you."

"Chipped!" Zeus hollers. Yes. *Exactly*.

Horrified, Jin stares at the bracelet. "I just . . . wanted him to like me again," Jin whispers. "To see that I wasn't a loser. To see how okay I was even without him. And he did *this*?" His limbs go loose, and for a second, I think he might collapse in a heap. Instead, he frantically begins pulling on the bracelet until the woven strands snap, and he hurls it into the river.

"I can't believe you," Hannah says. "You ruined everything!" We were so close. I had the Helm in my hands. I had our way back onto the Task Force. My head swims.

"I'm so sorry," Jin mutters. "If I could take it all back, I would."

"Well, we don't have a time machine," Hannah snarls, "so that is not happening."

"I said I was sorry."

"Those are just *words*."

Okay, Lola. Get a grip. The sign of a good leader is that she doesn't go to pieces when things turn bad. She is tenacious. She does not quit.

And this is a time when I need to be that leader. I take a deep breath. We can be mad at Jin later for making poor choices, but right now we have another problem. How to steal *back* what was stolen from us.

"You guys," I interrupt. "Enough! If we want to get the Helm, we can't sit here arguing all night."

They both shut up and glare at me, which makes no sense because I have done nothing wrong other than allow the Helm to be taken right out of my hands. In my defense, I was distracted at the time by potentially drowning.

"What does it look like?" Jin asks tentatively. "The Helm, I mean?"

"Oh, it's a beautiful gold crown," replies Hannah, "embedded with rubies and diamonds."

"Really?"

"No," Hannah snaps. "It's a baseball hat. *Where* do we find Paul? Where does he live?"

Even if we can find Paul, we can't get to him. We are stuck on an island in the middle of the night with no boat. "I don't know his address," Jin says. "I only know the name of his town."

"Chappaqua," I mutter. Not helpful. Jin's shoulders sag. He's diminished, looking like he might shrivel up and blow away on the next strong breeze.

My heart sinks, and the nauseous ache of failure settles right in my core. I take a deep, hiccuping inhale, afraid that I might start to cry again, and when I do, I catch the faint scent of . . . lavender.

CHAPTER 37

THE SWEET SMELL OF SUCCESS

I HOLD UP A HAND TO SILENCE JIN AND HANNAH. "Do you smell that?" I whisper. "Lavender."

"Huh?" Jin glances around, unsure what is happening. But Hannah gets it right away, sniffing the air and grinning.

"They must be here," she says. "The Chappaqua boys."

"Oh," Jin says finally. "The *bandanna*. They took it?"

I nod. Of course, they have the Helm, so we can't see them, but because we can *smell* them, I assume they are nearby and can see us. "Keep talking," I say. "Act normal." Whatever that is.

Clearing my head, I take a deep breath. The lavender scent comes from over my right shoulder. Slowly, I inch the group in that direction, wondering how exactly we are supposed to take back something we cannot see. For now, we will have to settle for getting closer. We creep along in the direction of what I think is the group of boys, all the while chattering away about how we might, someday, get off this island.

The floral scent intensifies. They are close. Why can't we hear them? Does the Helm provide a bubble of silence, too? That would be unfair. This entire situation is unfair! We traded for the Helm, straight up, and Paul and his horrible posse of idiot friends stole it from us. At this moment I'd like nothing more than to kick Paul into the harbor.

The lavender scent is strong now. They must be right here. It occurs to me that they are messing with us, but that is not surprising. It's what they have been doing all along. I'll admit, it troubles me to think we were so easily fooled. They took the Helm right out of my *hands*. I might never get over that.

I'm in the middle of this ugly thought when suddenly, I'm sure someone is breathing down my neck. Like, *literally*. It is hot and steaming and smells of barbecue potato chips eaten sometime in the last few hours. Another reason I don't like these kids! Why ruin a perfectly good potato chip with bizarre orange flavoring that stains your fingers and tastes like feet? It takes all my willpower not to reel around and grab whoever it is. Using only my eyes, I try to communicate to Jin and Hannah that our adversaries are directly behind me.

"Do you have something stuck in your eye?" Jin asks. "Want me to take a look?"

"They are *right there*," I hiss, jabbing my thumb in their direction. Without missing a beat, Hannah launches herself into the air, her arms flailing in loopy circles as she flies.

"Hannah!" Jin yells. But she doesn't land on the hard ground. Instead, she collides with bodies we cannot see, arms still swinging wildly. Someone yelps in surprise. Now on the ground, Hannah sweeps her legs side to side, and the boys tumble around her.

But as they tumble around her, suddenly we can *see* them, three boys in Chappaqua Country Day T-shirts. It worked! Paul is the one with my bandanna tied around his neck, the fan blowing his shaggy bangs straight up in the air. The second boy is Barf Boy from the barge, and the third wears soggy checkerboard Vans. I take in these details in a hot second as the baseball hat of invisibility, knocked off Paul's head, sails into the air. As Jin and I lunge for it at the same time, we collide, and the hat falls from the sky right back into Paul's hands. No!

"Nice try, suckers!" he yells, pulling it tight on his head and instantly vanishing.

Vans and Barf Boy spin wildly, looking for him. "Paul! Where are you? Grab our hands! They can see us!"

"Ben can come," Paul says gleefully. And in a flash, Barf Boy disappears. "Daniel, you're fired. You were never really into this anyway. And you whine and complain all the time about everything. It's a total downer."

"What? You can't do that!" Daniel howls. "How am I going to get home?"

"Don't know. Don't care! Later, loser!" I imagine Paul dancing around like a maniac, dizzy with his new power.

"I don't know if this is a good idea, Paul." This comes from Ben, his voice heavy with doubt. "There aren't any other boats here. He's going to get in trouble if he gets caught."

"*When* he gets caught." Paul snickers. "Daniel, remember when I was new at school and you wouldn't let me sit at your table? I wasn't cool enough for you. You called me Puny Paul. You laughed at me. But who's laughing *now*? Who's cool *now*? You guys were pathetic before me."

An eerie silence settles over the boys. Daniel stares into the darkness, bewildered. "Ben, you can't let him do this," he says.

"But Ben isn't in charge, is he?" Paul replies icily. "Are you, Ben?"

"No," Ben whispers.

"If you want to stay behind with Daniel, a happy little loser twosome, you totally can. Make your choice."

There is a long pause, during which I think Ben might decide to bolt. But he doesn't. "I'm in," he says. "I am. Bye, loser Daniel."

Moments later, we are greeted by the almost imperceptible sound of an electric boat engine starting up. Daniel blanches. "He took the boat and *left* me here," he mutters. "I can't believe it."

You better believe it! And why are you surprised? Paul is the worst friend in the history of friends. How did you not see that coming? But I will give Paul credit. He has a weird power over people, like Jin, who was willing to do anything to get his attention.

Emerging from the shadows, we race to the water's edge in time to see an empty black escape raft puttering away into the darkness.

"I am getting really sick of him," Hannah growls. "And why didn't *we* think to tie up at least one of our rafts?"

Jin sputters out some explanation about how his knot-tying ability is not world-class, but Hannah is not listening. She charges back to Daniel, who is now forlorn *and* totally confused.

"Aren't you the ones from the Midnight Market?" he asks. "Who we took that invisibility baseball hat from, right? What are you doing here?"

Hannah is toe-to-toe with him. "What are *we* doing here?" she bellows. "What do you *think* we are doing here? You stole our Helm! Tell me where your friends are going right now, or I will dedicate the rest of my life to ruining yours."

"She's totally not kidding," Jin says. Daniel's face collapses. He is close to tears. I remind myself that he was part of the gang that mugged me when I was drowning. He is not a friend, but wet and bedraggled, he doesn't look like much of an adversary right now either.

"Paul said he wanted to go into the torch of the Statue of Liberty because it is off-limits," Daniel says. "You know, illegal and stuff. That's where they are probably going."

We stare into the night toward Liberty Island, which is close but also not. "Let's swim it," Hannah suggests. "We are getting that Helm back no matter what."

"It's too far," Daniel points out. "You won't make it."

"Be quiet," I snap. But he's right. "It's too far. We won't make it."

Does this mean our hunt ends in defeat? Does Paul *win*? Do we return empty-handed, complete failures who will be instantly kicked out of camp for going rogue? I can tell I'm running on pure adrenaline because random thoughts keep intruding, including what it must be like to live inside Paul's head. How anxious and uncomfortable to always have to pretend you are something other than what you are. Why would you want to be friends with people who don't like you? I also think about waffles dripping with butter and maple syrup. My hands squeeze the princess crystals in my pocket.

Wait. The princess crystals!

"You guys!" I pull them out and hold them up. "Look!"

"You *stole* princess crystals?" Hannah asks, aghast. "I thought you said your life of crime was behind you?"

"Princess who?" Jin looks back and forth between us.

"No, I didn't steal them! Sparkle Lady gave them to me right before we jumped overboard. She said they might come in handy."

"Can someone please explain?" Jin demands.

"Princess crystals," I say. "They can be magical, I guess? You can make wishes but only small, simple ones." I hold up one of the crystals. It's like a snow globe full of silver glitter, but the glitter swirls and swims in an unearthly substance. Definitely not liquid, almost like fog. And it glows faintly. I give it a little shake. "Like, how about I wish for a boat to bring us to the Statue of Liberty?"

"And the boat is loaded with snacks," Jin adds quickly. "For us and Zeus."

"Snacks!" Zeus bellows. Of course, nothing happens. Did I really think it would?

"Try again," urges Hannah. "Sometimes these magical objects are finicky, you know?"

I shake the glass ball again. Streaks of silver swirl in the fog, and the ball grows warm in my hand. And almost soft, like the hard glass shell has turned to squishy rubber. "I'd like a boat full of snacks to take us to the Statue of Liberty, please."

"You have to say 'wish,'" Jin whispers. I do? How does he know? Who made him the princess-crystal expert?

I clear my throat. "Sorry. I mean I *wish* for a boat full of snacks to take us to the Statue of Liberty. Please. And thank you. And have a good day. Or technically, night, I guess. Oh boy."

We wait, a little breathless, in the eerie silence. But nothing happens. Suddenly I feel ridiculous. "This is stupid," I say, throwing the princess crystal at the ground. It hits, exploding in a cloud of silver sparks. And in the distance, an engine hums. Bright lights appear on the water.

A glittery glowing boat, not much bigger than the rubber rafts, glides gently to a smooth stop right at the water's edge. There is no driver. Tendrils of fog rise up and wrap around us, urging us forward.

"Look," Jin says with awe. Stacked in the bottom is a smorgasbord of snacks. There are Goldfish crackers, Twizzlers, shiny purple plums, granola bars, packets of applesauce, a box of Oreos, and a bag of kale bits for Zeus.

"Take me with you!" Daniel pleads as we climb aboard. "You can't leave me here!"

Jin looks at him sadly. "Sorry you had to learn the hard way," he says quietly. "But take it from me. Next time choose better friends. It makes all the difference. And you'll be fine—the tourists show up pretty early in the morning. Now come on, guys. There is treasure hunting that needs doing."

Without looking back, Jin jumps into the boat, which reverses into the water. And off we go, wrapped in magic we can't even begin to understand.

CHAPTER 38

LADY LIBERTY, HERE WE COME!

IT DOES NOT TAKE LONG TO REACH LIBERTY ISLAND, but it's enough time for us to demolish the snacks. Zeus murmurs happily on Jin's shoulder. Grateful for my second wind, I jump out prepared to do battle for the Helm, Jin and Hannah by my side. I'd like to ask the boat to wait for us, but I don't want to overstep the bounds of a single princess crystal. They are sensitive, according to the Midnight Market lady with no teeth.

We stalk the statue in total stealth mode but, apparently, we are not that good at it because we get caught before a single minute goes by.

"Hey, you kids! What are you doing? Freeze!" Uh-oh.

Paul is invisible. We, on the other hand, are not. A guard in a navy-blue uniform trundles over to us.

"We can outrun him," Hannah whispers. "He's out of shape."

"We're on an island," Jin replies. "Where are we going to go?" Both are excellent points. And I have an idea. Quickly, I pull a smoke-bomb Ping-Pong ball from my backpack.

"Follow my lead," I say, and hurl the ball at the guard's feet. Immediately, it engulfs him in a cloud of smoke. Yes! My smoke bomb works even when wet! The guard coughs and waves his hands around to clear the air. It's time to run. "To the statue!"

We bolt toward the base of Lady Liberty. The guard, coughing and cursing, stumbles after us. There's a row of garbage cans off to the side of the path, and hunkered down behind them, we listen as the guard approaches.

"Don't even breathe," I whisper.

"You don't need to tell us that," Hannah shoots back.

"I'm talking to the bird," I reply.

"Oh. Yeah." But Zeus has his head tucked beneath his wing. How can he sleep at a moment like this? Muttering angrily, the guard waves his flashlight around, hoping to catch a glimpse of us. We stay very still. My leg starts to cramp and my toes tingle. Jin wiggles his elbow and gets me between the rib cage. Hannah sighs to indicate she is highly disappointed at our lack of discipline.

Obviously convinced we were a trick of his imagination, the guard gives up and trudges away. We wait until we can no longer see his rumpled form before creeping out from behind the garbage cans.

Along the backside of the statue's pedestal, there is an AUTHORIZED PERSONNEL ONLY door cracked open. This must be how Paul and Ben slipped inside. Following their lead, we squeeze through, careful to keep our footsteps quiet. A narrow hall deposits us in the main lobby, where the original torch, replaced after an explosion, sits front and center. And while it is meant to be inspiring, in the dim light, everything appears ominous. Where are they? Are they watching us right now? This invisibility thing sure is a pain in the neck.

But my brain is busy compensating, replacing sight with smell. The hint of lavender in the air promises we are on the right track. We follow our noses and climb 192 steps to the pedestal viewing area. Bathed in sweat, we squat low on the stairs and listen.

"I want to climb out on the crown," Paul says. "You know, like out the window. It will be so rad. Completely dangerous. The best!" He laughs. It is a frantic, high-pitched sound that has nothing to do with joy or fun. Jin cringes.

"That's crazy," Ben replies. "It's a twenty-two-story building, and I don't think there is a ledge."

"I regret inviting you along already," Paul says dismissively. There is a scuffle, and suddenly Ben appears on the landing.

"Hey," Ben protests. "You let me go. You can't do that."

"Can and did," replies Paul. "Something you should remember. How much trouble would you be in if they found you here in the morning? My guess is a lot." He chuckles to himself, as if this game he is playing is just the most fun ever.

"I'm in," Ben says. "I told you that already. Let's go." Suddenly he's gone again. There is the echo of footsteps as the invisible pair departs. Behind them, we sneak along and make our way to the stairs that lead to the crown.

Staying back and out of sight, we begin to climb the 192 steps to the crown. The stairway is narrow, steep, and dark. I have to concentrate to keep from tripping over my own feet.

The inside of Lady Liberty's crown is like the inside of a skull, a web of structural metal beams keeping it from caving in. It's a tight space, so we hide in the shadows. Up ahead, one of the oblong windows, about as wide as my shoulders, opens, and Ben appears. Paul has released him.

"Go," Paul commands. "Climb out. See what it's like."

The fear on Ben's face is obvious, even from where we crouch. Climbing out there is insane. And pointless. In this moment, I understand why the Task Force works so hard to keep magical mythical potentially dangerous treasures out of the hands of regular everyday people. It is because regular everyday people cannot handle the power. They do dumb things, dangerous things, and just like that, a kid is climbing out a window almost three hundred feet above the ground. Ben, face contorted, sweat rolling down from his temples, gives in to the bullying and wedges himself through the window.

I don't think we can actually sit here and watch this happen. But as I'm about to reveal myself, Hannah leaps to her feet and charges the window.

"Don't! Stop!" she yells. In his surprise, Ben slips and pitches headlong out the window. Hannah screams and flies through the air, catching him by the ankle. But his weight pulls her forward, and while her feet scramble to find purchase, there is none to be had. I get ahold of her shirt a split second before she disappears over the edge.

"Lola!"

"I've got you! Don't let go! Jin, find something, a rope, anything!"

As Jin scrambles, Paul laughs and laughs. "Look who

showed up," he cackles. "My friends. Or whatever you are. Oh, wait. I know what you are. You are no fun."

Hannah's shirt tears in my hand. "Jin!"

He's at my side, breathing hard. "There's nothing. I can't find anything."

The shirt is not going to hold, and Jin can't help me hold on because the window is too narrow for both of us to fit.

Think, Lola! There is no way you let this happen.

"Jin! In my pocket, the other princess crystal! Grab it!" Jin produces the crystal and holds it up. I can't let go of the shirt or they fall, so I send a silent hope into the universe that this crystal likes Jin well enough to grant him his wish. "Wish for a soft landing," I whisper, sweat pouring down my face. And in that moment, the shirt gives and Hannah and Ben plummet to the earth. Jin smashes the princess crystal and screams. I scream. Zeus screams.

But an amazing thing happens below. The ground appears to undulate like a wave building momentum. It rises up to the falling bodies and catches them gently in a pocket of soft green grass, holding them safe and tight as it settles once again into a flat lawn. Hannah and Ben are sprawled on the grass almost three hundred feet below. Unharmed.

"What was *that*?" Paul asks accusingly. "You never mentioned *that*, Jin."

"The Helm belongs to *us*," I say. I pull myself back into the room, my eyes tracking his voice. "It's not a toy. It's dangerous."

"Don't try to scare me," Paul says. "You think you're so special, with your fancy STEM fair projects and Jin thinking you're amazing and all that. Really, you are just some *girl*."

I don't like the way he says that. It makes my eyebrow twitch.

"She is not," Jin replies. "I mean, yes she is a girl, but Lola is my *best* friend." I can't see Paul, but I swear I can hear him stiffen. "She's everything you aren't. Reliable. Trustworthy. Encouraging. Nice. Funny. Jeez, I can't even remember why I liked you!"

"Shut. Up." Paul has moved closer to Jin. "Don't say another word."

"Why?" Jin demands. "Because if I do, you will throw me out a window? Who *does* that to their friends?" I realize that I have never seen Jin truly angry. And right now, he is raging. "You are a pathetic, sad person. And desperate, too. And lame. And . . ."

Jin should have stopped at pathetic. Midsentence Zeus is knocked off his shoulder, and Jin is thrown to the floor by our invisible adversary. His head hits the ground hard.

It sounds like a melon rolling off a table. I crawl toward him, but Paul shoves me back. "This is all your fault," Paul hisses. "I think you should go out the window too, and I bet you don't have any more of those magic crystal balls to save you."

He grabs my leg in an attempt to drag me toward the window, but I kick free, get to my feet, and run the only direction I can, through the barrier and up the ladder toward the torch, clutched in Lady Liberty's eternal grip.

CHAPTER 39

INTO THE FIRE

LADY LIBERTY'S TORCH WAS CLOSED TO VISITORS in 1916, after an explosion on Black Tom Island in New York Harbor in the middle of the night sent shrapnel flying into the arm and torch of the statue, damaging it. In 1986, the arm was repaired and the torch replaced, with a copper flame covered in 24K gold. Despite the repairs, it was never again reopened to tourists and I can see why. The forty-foot ladder, which workers use to maintain the floodlights that illuminate the torch, rises in the tight narrow shaft of the arm. It's barely the width of my shoulders. Were people smaller when they built this thing?

I can't see Paul, but I can hear his labored breathing

right at my heels. I urge my legs to go faster. But what do I do at the top? Panic? Scream? Grow wings and fly? If only I had more princess crystals!

It's okay, Lola. You will figure it out.

Boy, I hope so. Remind me why I wanted to hunt for missing magical mythical potentially dangerous treasures again? Yeah. I don't know the answer to that. At the top, I shove open the hatch to the small deck surrounding the flame. Flooded with light, it really looks like it's on fire! It's so beautiful I want to stop and admire it, but this is no time for a scenic tour. I slam the hatch shut behind me and scurry to the far side, putting the flame between me and Paul.

Now what? There is no way off other than the ladder. I slide to the ground, resting my forehead on my knees. I am all *alone*. No one is coming to save me. Sure, my friends like me, but to follow me up here where I'm trapped with a lunatic—does our friendship go that far, that deep? I mean, even Zeus has abandoned me. And anyway, this mess is all my fault. Going rogue was my idea. Hiding Lipstick's involvement is all on me too.

Beside me is a bucket of water and a few dried-out sponges, probably used to clean the many floodlights, and not deep enough for me to submerge myself and disappear. I'm doomed. That's it. Might as well accept it. I tried to be a treasure hunter, but I failed and let everyone down in the process. The hatch clatters open, and the smell of lavender wafts through the air. Oh wait. Maybe I have an idea after all.

"You stole my bandanna," I say, feeling Paul's eyes on me even if I can't see him. "And you ghosted Jin. Neither of those things is very nice." If I can get him talking, I can follow his voice. Maybe I can tangle up his legs and knock him over long enough to take the Helm and escape down the ladder. It's not much of a plan, but it will have to do. "Why would you do that? He was a good friend to you, and good friends are hard to come by."

Silence. Okay. Fine. I can keep talking, just watch.

"But really, you weren't worthy of him," I continue. From what I've seen, Paul has a short fuse, so making him jealous might be the best way to get him to speak up. "He is way cooler than you are. I mean, the Task Force was falling all over itself trying to get him on board. He's a natural, a gifted treasure hunter. Like, maybe the best ever. A total GOAT. A *legend*."

"He's not the greatest of all time," Paul says. "Give me a break." Boom! Did it! He's close, coming up on my left side. I slide my legs under me so I'm ready to spring at him.

"One in a million," I say. "Everyone is going to be doing things Jin's way in no time at all. I, for one, am dazzled."

"You're lying." He's so close I can feel his breath on my skin. This is it. One step closer.

"Am I?"

With that, I spring at him like a coiled jack-in-the-box clown. But I land flat on my face, smashing my elbow hard on the ground. Paul's laughter fills the air. "Nice try. Can't see me. Can't catch me. Now, I think I'm going to leave you up here. Jam that hatch shut and see how long you last. That would be fun. And funny. And you *deserve* it."

"The Helm will make you do things you regret," I say with a groan. I remember how possessed I felt by the Stone of Istenanya, when it whispered to me about all the power I could have, and how much in that moment, I wanted that power. Is Paul being corrupted by the Helm's power, or is he just a jerk?

"I regret nothing." He smirks. Yup. Just a jerk. "Anyway, gotta run. Banks to rob and stuff." I rub my tired eyes, and when I open them, I catch a flash of something by the hatch.

Hannah! Quiet as a ghost, she climbs out, followed by Jin. They came to help me! Hope surges. This is *not* over.

"Banks?" I say quickly, trying to keep Paul's attention

on me. "That's your big play? How cliché! Wow. Way to waste a superpower."

"Huh?"

"You heard me. Boring with a capital *B*."

"And what are you, like, an expert?" His voice keeps moving, like he's pacing the small space, but this makes it hard to nail him down. If we make a move and fail, he can easily hop down the ladder and make his getaway with the Helm.

"Pretty close," I say. "I have quite a bit of experience with magical objects. More than you, anyway." Jin and Hannah come from different directions. Suddenly, Jin yelps with pain.

"Ow! My shin! He kicked me!"

"Where is he?" I yell.

"I don't know!" Hannah shouts back. We swing our arms wildly, hoping to make contact, but Paul is *nowhere*. If only we could see him, this would be so much easier!

Oh, but maybe we *can*. Dorothy tossed a bucket of water on the Wicked Witch of the West and steamed her to death, but I want to *see* Paul. Quickly, I grab the water bucket with two hands and heave the contents into the air. As the water rains down, like a summer cloudburst, there is the shimmery outline of Paul, crawling toward the hatch. And that is the exact moment Zeus swoops in, snatches the Helm right off his head, and flies out of the crown.

Face scrunched with fury, Paul lunges after Zeus and tips dangerously over the edge of the torch. At the last second, Jin grabs his old friend by the waistband, pulling him back to safety. They tumble in a heap to the ground.

"What happened?" Paul cries.

"You lost," Jin says.

CHAPTER 40

ARE WATER TAXIS A THING?

SIRENS BLARE AND POLICE BOATS FLY ACROSS THE water as we scramble down the ladder and the stairs and out of the Statue of Liberty. The grounds are flooded with security. Did the guard realize he wasn't dreaming and call for help? Did he see the ground rise up to catch Hannah and Ben? There is a lot of screaming when we are spotted fleeing the landmark.

"Zeus! The Helm!" There is a split-second pause, during which I wonder if Zeus has gone power mad too. I could see it happening. "*Now*, Zeus!" He deposits the mythical cap on my head and perches on my shoulder. Pulling the cap secure, I grab my friends.

And we vanish.

It feels weird. Tingly almost, like I'm being stung by a thousand tiny well-meaning jellyfish. And I'm lighter, too, like gravity isn't working right. Are my feet even touching the ground? The security guards and the police pull to an abrupt stop.

A refrain of "Where are they? Where did they go?" rings out across the lawn. Hands clutched tight, we move slowly and deliberately toward the water. We have no boat and no way off this island, but if we stay invisible, we can simply sneak onto a ferry in the morning. No one has to know.

Being invisible is wild. I get the appeal. Not that I'd rob a bank or anything. No. I'd go directly to the Louvre and lift the *Mona Lisa*. Just kidding. Or maybe I'm not.

I'm busy reminding myself not to get swept up in the Helm's power when Hannah nudges me. *"Look,"* she says. Rushing in our direction, almost as if he can *see* us, is my dad, but he's dressed in a suit and has a badge dangling from his neck. He stops a group of uniformed cops, and they gesture and point and shrug, and he nods and pats one of them on the shoulder as if they are good friends. He then proceeds toward us, stopping about ten feet away, hands on hips, scowling and scanning the grounds.

"Dad!"

His head darts around, searching us out. "Where are you?" he asks. "Do you realize half the New York City Police Department is searching for you? They found a kid on Ellis Island who told quite a tale. Now, take me into your invisibility bubble because this badge is fake and I don't want to go to jail. I've heard the food is wretched in the clink."

I pull Dad in close and breathe in the smell of him. He's an unconventional father, to be sure, but I wouldn't want it any other way. "Thank you for coming."

"I'd have been here sooner except Zeus's chip seems to be no longer functioning. Naughty Zeus." Zeus hangs his head but also smirks. Typical Zeus. "I had to track the police scanner, but as soon as I heard the details from the Ellis Island boy—magic crystal balls, the power of invisibility—I knew right away where to find you. I *never* should have left you in Grand Central, but I thought . . . Well, never mind what I thought. Let's find where I left that boat and get out of here."

Once we are safely on board Dad's boat and clear from the shore, I remove the cap and we let go of one another's hands. My friends come into quick relief.

"Good to see you," Jin says with a sly grin.

Hannah snorts with laughter. "You too."

I want to ask Jin if he is okay, if Paul doing what he did left yet another hole in his heart, but he beats me to it. "You guys are the best friends a person could want," he says quietly. "And I'm sorry I let you down. It won't happen again."

"It better not," Hannah snaps.

I pat Jin on the thigh. "It's okay. We're more than our mistakes, right? At least that's what Judge Gold told me. Several times."

"Will they let us back on the Task Force now?" Hannah asks.

"They have to, don't they?" Jin adds.

We all look to Dad, who mans the wheel. "I'm sure," he says. But I will only believe it when I see it, and I've learned a thing or two about what can be seen and what can't be in the last twenty-four hours.

Dad captains us directly to the airport. We stride across the tarmac like we own the place, which cannot be legal, toward a small prop plane. "Now, listen up, team," Dad says. "This is your ride back to camp, where you will rendezvous with Star and Fish. I told them you had something for them, but I didn't say what. I thought the element of surprise might be fun. I will see you at the conclusion of camp."

"You're not coming?" I ask.

A dark look clouds his face. "There's something I need to do that is rather . . . urgent in nature."

"What?"

But before he can answer, the plane's engines roar to life, and my voice is drowned out. Dad grins and gives us a thumbs-up and shoves us up the stairs into the cabin. He has to stop popping off like this. I have a lot of questions!

We settle in, suddenly exhausted from twenty-four hours of madness. The weariness seeps into my bones, and my eyelids droop. As the wheels come up, the Helm clutched tight in my hand, just before we fall asleep, I whisper, "Thank you for rescuing me in the torch."

And my friends whisper back, "It's what friends do, Lola."

I dream of Star and Fish, humbled and grateful, begging us to share treasure-hunting tips. There is an unknown mayor giving us the key to his unknown city. There is Sparkle Lady patting me on the back. Wait. What is she doing here? *Okay.* I'll deal with that later. Moving on. There is my father, beaming with pride and introducing me to his friends as Lola Benko, *treasure hunter.*

By the time we make it to Timber Wolf Island, I'm fully awake, and twitchy with nervousness even though we have the Helm and as far as anyone at camp knows, we were taking Zeus to the parrot veterinarian in New York City. Lipstick aside, of course.

It's already hot and sticky outside. Flies swarm my head. Zeus snores happily in Jin's pocket. Squinting into the sun, I see Lipstick waiting for us onshore. No gnat or fly would dare buzz her head. There is no sign of Moose. My foot taps in a puddle of oil and water collected in the bottom of the boat. I squeeze the Helm in my pocket.

"Campers," Lipstick says, her eyes shaded by big round sunglasses. "How delightful to see you again. I assume Zeus is well?"

"He's fine," I say.

"Wonderful. Such *good* news. Now, come with me, kids," she says coolly. "We must get you all caught up. I'll see to it that the cafeteria whips up some lunch for you travelers. You must be starved." As we head for her office, clusters of campers turn out to stare at us, like we are walking to an execution. I can imagine the rumors that arose from our sudden disappearance.

It's dark in Lipstick's office, and she does not invite us to sit on the uncomfortable couch. Although we slept on the short plane ride, the fatigue is dulling my wits. All the lights are surrounded by halos, as if I have spent too much time underwater. And my mouth tastes like dried crickets, which Dad made me try once when we were in Thailand. For the record, not my favorite snack.

As Lipstick settles in behind her desk, her expression shifts from determined, her normal state, to something almost *satisfied*. The only reason I notice is because it is the same expression I remember from when we first saw her with my dad in the tunnels under San Francisco. She had my dad and she had the Stone of Istenanya. She had everything she wanted. A chill runs up my spine despite the heat. I clutch the hat tighter.

"Do you have it?" she asks.

Jin and Hannah stare at me, shocked, as I pull out the hat. Lipstick exhales slowly. "Remarkable." Not so bad for your inelegant, messy, impulsive last choice, Lipstick! "I must admit your initiative was impressive. I think it bodes well for your future. Most kids wanted to figure out the location of the Midnight Market, but you actually attended and succeeded."

She eyes us, a challenge to admit how we ended up finding the market in the first place. I look at my feet. Jin looks at the ceiling. Hannah examines her cuticles.

"And it really works?" Lipstick asks. For a flash, I think she's going to ask to try it on and, oh, I really don't want that to happen! Lipstick is not to be trusted. But instead, she insists I demonstrate.

Pulling off my watch, I hold it up for her to see. The face is black as if it burned up inside. I lay it on her desk. "Wearing the Helm fries your electronics," I explain. "It ruined my watch."

She cocks her head to one side. "Of course. *So* interesting."

"Okay. Here we go." I push back my hair and slap the hat on my head.

The kitten paws and jellyfish are all over me. I shiver and twitch. Lipstick's grin is almost as wide as her face.

"What a wonderful magical treasure," she purrs. And that's when I'm absolutely positively one hundred percent sure I'm missing something. This is about more than her wanting to outdo an adversary, to thwart a nemesis. I just don't know what it *is*.

CHAPTER 41

LIPSTICK PULLS A FAST ONE

JIN POKES AT ME WITH A FINGER. "WOW. IT'S STILL so weird. I don't think I'm ever going to get used to this."

"Lola?" Zeus squawks with some urgency. I wonder if baby birds develop object permanence like baby humans. It might explain why Zeus sounds worried that I might have vanished forever.

"I'm here," I say, pulling the hat off.

"Lola!" I give Zeus a quick scratch under his feathery chin.

"Would you like me to hold on to the hat for you?" Lipstick asks, narrowing her gaze. "Keep it safe until the Task Force arrives to relieve us of it?"

"No!" My answer comes fast from my gut. No way! Never! I don't feel attached to the hat like I did to the Stone of Istenanya. It's not emotionally manipulating me, but I still feel the overwhelming urge to hang on to it tight. It's a hat that disappears, so I don't think my anxiety is misplaced. Plus, this is *Lipstick* we are talking about.

"Very well," Lipstick says curtly. "Your father took the liberty of informing Star and Fish that you had something you wished to share with them. They are en route and should arrive in due time. Until then, keep that hat in a safe place. You are free to rejoin camp activities, but may I suggest a shower first?" She turns up her nose. Yes. We know. Imagine how bad it would be if I hadn't taken that dip in the Hudson River last night.

"Dismissed." And with that, Lipstick waves us away. If this was about taking the Helm, wouldn't she have done it? Is it possible she is telling the truth about her nemesis? Until I know for sure, I will keep one hand on the Helm at all times.

Over lunch, Jin and Hannah puzzle over who helped us. Who arranged for us to get the clue? Who sent us to New York City? Who gave us the gold bar? Lipstick. Lipstick. Lipstick. That's who. We were out treasure hunting *for* her *because* of her.

"I have to tell you something," I say, my throat tight. "It's bad."

"Worse than Jin being spied on by Paul?" Hannah asks, cramming a bite of peanut butter and jelly in her mouth.

"You are never going to let me live that down, are you?" Jin shoots back.

"Nope. Never. What is it, Lola? You look weird."

"Lipstick offered me a deal. It was the middle of the night. She said we were in a giant treasure-hunting hole, and if we ever wanted to get out, we had to go big. She's the one who helped us. But only because she didn't want her nemesis to get the Helm. It wasn't Star and Fish thinking we are awesome. It was all Lipstick." Every last bit.

"Why didn't you tell us?" Jin asks quietly.

"I wanted to," I say. "And I tried, but I guess I didn't try hard enough. I'm sorry."

They stare at me for a long hot terrible moment and I cannot even guess what they are thinking, until Jin breaks the silence.

"I guess we've all done things since the Pegasus disaster," he says. "You know, stuff that is not so great. Paul. Lipstick."

"Not me," Hannah interrupts. "I didn't do anything."

"You *ditched* us," Jin says pointedly. "You said we were

boring. You were with Bodhi *all the time*. You needed your adrenaline rush or whatever." Oh. So I guess he *did* notice.

Hannah eyes us cautiously. "Did I really say you were boring?"

"You did," I respond.

"And I really blew you off?"

"Yes," Jin replies.

She glances from me to Jin. "I didn't realize," she says. "I'm sorry, but why didn't you tell me I was acting like a jerk?"

That's a fine question. Why *didn't* I say something to my friends when I was feeling bad? Why didn't I trust them enough? "I don't know," I say. "You *said* we were boring. And we know that's like the kiss of death for you."

Hannah cocks her head to the left. "For the record," she says, "Bodhi is fun and all, but he's not you guys. There's nothing I wouldn't do for this team. Nothing. Besides, just yesterday I fell out of the Statue of Liberty and was rescued when the grass came to life and saved me. So. Not. Boring."

"That really happened," Jin muses.

"It totally did," I say.

"I can't believe Lipstick has a *nemesis*," Hannah adds, shaking her head. "How truly terrifying."

And in the silence that follows, I feel for the first time that maybe we have moved past where we were and to a place that is better and stronger. It could happen. It might be real.

The rest of the day passes in a blur of exhausted contentment, and we collapse into bed while the sun is still bright. My legs are leaden and my head feels clogged with cotton. In the other room, Jin whispers to Zeus, "You're a good bird. A smart bird. A pretty bird." And Zeus whispers back, "Snacks?"

I fall asleep smiling, to the quiet snores of Hannah in the top bunk, the hat stuffed in my pillowcase tucked under my head.

We *did* it. Everything worked out exactly as I hoped.

My dreams are full of rain and thunder, as if the world outside has gone mad, but when I wake up, all I hear is the symphony of crickets. The bedroom window is streaked with rivulets, glistening in the moonlight. I stretch and yawn and reach into the pillowcase to give the Helm of Darkness a squeeze.

But it's *gone*.

Immediately, my heart shifts into overdrive and adrenaline floods my system. Leaping from bed, I search everywhere, but there is no sign of the hat. Maybe the hat put itself on and disappeared? Is that possible?

No, Lola. A hat can't wear itself.

"Hannah! Wake up!" I shake her bed violently, and she opens one eye.

"What is wrong with you?" she groans.

"The Helm. I can't find it!" This gets her out of bed in a hurry. She searches everywhere I already did, despite my telling her so.

"It's gone," she says breathlessly.

"That's what I *told* you."

There is a flash of lightning and a clap of thunder followed by a shriek, the human kind, the Jin kind. "Lola! Hannah! Get out here!" Maybe he found the Helm? Hannah and I try to cram through the door at the same time, and smash shoulders and get stuck. "Go," I say, an acid taste on my tongue that I recognize as fear. Tomorrow was supposed to be about our glory! This cannot be happening again. This is so not glorious.

"Oh wow." Hannah stops abruptly, and I plow into her. "Look at *that*." On the tree-stump coffee table lies a necklace, glittering with the most beautiful gems I've ever seen, strung together with delicate rose-gold links as if by magic. It's nestled in a dark-blue velvet box, under which is tucked an envelope.

"*What* is it?" Jin asks anxiously. "*Why* is it here?" Zeus flutters to the necklace and pecks it a few times to determine if it falls into the snack category. Deciding not so much, he heads to the windowsill to peer out into the night.

As I reach for the envelope, it starts to come together in my head. But it can't be. I refuse to accept the possibility. "*Read* it," Hannah says sharply, circling the coffee table cautiously like the necklace might ignite. I open the envelope and pull out the card, written on thick, creamy stationery. The words are in a tight looping hand.

"I meant to teach you a lesson," I read aloud, *"specifically, that payback hurts, that there is nothing in the world that I cannot take from you, that you are nothing special. But perhaps I was wrong. This is NOT an apology. Rather, I consider it a fair trade, proper payment for a job well done. I hope our paths cross again in the future. In fact, I am sure they will."*

"Huh? I don't get it." Jin's eyebrows cut a deep crease in his forehead.

But I do. "The Helm is gone," I say. "Lipstick took it. She knew it would fry her ankle monitor and let her walk right out of here, undetected. Or swim? But more important, *that*"—I point to the box—"is the Pegasus necklace."

A fair trade, indeed.

CHAPTER 42

WHICH SUPERPOWER WOULD YOU PICK?

AT LEAST TWICE IN MIDDLE SCHOOL, I'VE BEEN asked the following question: If you could have the superpower of flight or invisibility, which would you choose? The question itself is not that interesting, but what *is* interesting is why people choose what they do.

Invisibility is never about saving the world. People don't say they want to help old ladies across the street or save cats stuck in trees or whatever. No way. What they want to do is sneak into the principal's office and change grades. Or spy on a best friend who is cheating with another friend they don't like that much. Or sneak into the movies without paying. Maybe grab an extra-large bucket of popcorn, and Junior Mints, too.

It's the same for flight. No one wants to pull a Superman. Instead, they want to get across the country fast without having to bother with the airport. Or maybe hover right above third base for the best view of the baseball game. How about avoiding traffic? Again, no world savers here.

But really, the question is a fantasy because no one ever *really* gets to choose. Well, most of the time anyway.

Star and Fish have arrived at Camp Timber Wolf, and while they are happy to have the necklace, they are unhappy about lots of other things. No one can find Lipstick. The International Task Force for the Cooperative Protection of Entities with Questionable Provenance has scrambled and sent a replacement, who should arrive by evening. Meanwhile, the campers run amuck. No one is in charge. And the cafeteria ran out of doughnuts. We are moments away from a full-on mutiny. It's all pretty funny, if you ask me, but not the doughnuts bit. That's a real problem.

Star and Fish manage to corral us into our cabin for interrogation. They claim they are doing nothing of the sort, but if it *sounds* like an interrogation and *feels* like an interrogation, it probably *is* an interrogation. They have a lot of questions, which they call "concerns," mostly that they know we were hunting the Helm but can't say so without getting in trouble themselves over Moose. And if we *were* hunting the Helm, why do we have the necklace instead? The whole tangled mess is stressing them out big-time.

"We were under the impression that you had attained the Helm of Darkness," Fish says through gritted teeth.

"Who said that?" I ask.

"Your *father*," Fish replies. "He instructed us to come here and get something from you."

"He did?" I ask, making my eyes wide.

"That Professor Benko," Hannah says, slapping her thigh. "A total trickster."

"Loves his practical jokes," Jin adds.

"He said you had something," Fish insists.

"Did he really?" I say quickly. "Because we *never* said that. And believe me, we would never say we had something when we didn't actually have it. Lesson learned."

"Seriously," Jin agrees. "Been there, done that, wasn't great."

"Did Moose tell you we had it?" Hannah asks. "Where is he anyway? He seems to have . . . disappeared." Fish turns a shade of green at the mention of Moose, which I enjoy immensely. After all, she told him to get rid of us. Not okay.

"We were here at camp the whole time," I add.

"Just ask the director," Jin volunteers. "Oh wait, you can't. She's gone."

Star and Fish seethe. "You kids . . ."

"Anyway, to be clear, we were definitely not out hunting some invisible hat thingy," I say.

Star tugs his bedraggled mustache. It looks like he did his grooming blindfolded. "It's not invisible," he says impatiently. "And it's not a *hat*."

"That's what you think," Jin replies under his breath.

"Jin!" Zeus caws, extra loud so Star and Fish jump in surprise.

"Shut that bird up," Fish barks.

"Rude!" sniffs Zeus, puffing his plumage.

"Okay. Fine," Fish says. "Then how and when did you come to possess the necklace?"

"I thought we were talking about hats?" Jin inquires.

"Besides, all necklace intelligence is classified," I say.

"Totally," Hannah agrees.

"As in, we could tell you, but then we'd have to kill you," Jin adds.

Fish grimaces. "Not funny, young man," she says.

Oh, it's definitely funny. Besides, everyone knows a good missing magical mythical potentially dangerous treasure hunter never gives up her sources.

"We need answers!" Star slams his hand on the table. "We know that you know *something* about *something.* Tell us *now*! I am not going back to Siberia!"

Huh? Who said anything about Siberia? This is getting out of hand. "Listen, you guys," I say. "We don't know about any Helm of Darkness. We didn't hunt it. We don't have it. But we *do* have the Pegasus necklace. We told you we'd get it and we *did*." It just took a little longer than expected.

"Yeah," Hannah agrees. "Take the necklace. It's yours. Hide it away in your vault or whatever. But can we hurry this up? It's almost lunchtime and I'm starved."

"I could murder a roast beef sandwich right now," Jin says.

"Fries," I add hopefully. "And ketchup."

"Can you stop talking about food and answer the question?" Star practically stomps his foot. He's grumpy enough that he could probably use some fries too. Seriously. Enough is enough.

"We have ten more days of camp left," I say, "and we'd like to have lunch before the afternoon's torture sessions begin."

"Team LJH is kicking butt, just FYI," Jin adds.

"We are *inevitable*," Hannah says, crossing her arms against her chest.

And it occurs to me that Lipstick *did* teach us a lesson by stealing Pegasus right out from under us in Morocco, but it was not the one she intended. She taught us that after getting knocked down, we alone are responsible for whether or not we stand back up. And not only did Team LJH stand back up, but we *roared*.

"Fine," Star says begrudgingly. "You can have your lunch and go do archery or horseback riding or whatever nonsense they have you doing out here. But first tell me one thing, and it better be the truth." His eyes narrow suspiciously. "Have you worn the necklace? Did you try it on?"

Did we wear the necklace? Did we try it on? What kind of questions are those?

What do you *think*?

CHAPTER 43

STAR AND FISH ARE FINALLY GETTING AHEAD

FISH: *They are lying. Those kids, I mean. They had the Helm. I know they did. And she stole it and escaped. But I still have no idea where the necklace came from. I hate surprises.*

STAR: *Any word on her?*

FISH: *Negative. She's vanished.*

STAR: *Well, I'd stop worrying. As long as she stays lost, we are okay. We definitely don't want to have to explain about the missing Moose. Besides, the Pegasus necklace is a major win for us. Can you believe how excited they were back at headquarters? They even said Egypt was "likely" in our future! Goodbye, Siberia!*

FISH: *I don't understand why they didn't ask more questions.*

They didn't even ask for the usual report. And they said nothing about the kids. Or about Moose being AWOL.

STAR: *I'm having a good day. Why are you determined to ruin it?*

FISH: *But it's weird, I tell you! Suspicious. There should be reams of paperwork associated with a find like this and there is exactly none. Something strange is going on.*

STAR: *You worry too much. Let it go! I'm going to surf the Mediterranean Sea! And we are going to get to treasure hunt some really stupendous things because of those kids—oh, wait—I mean, because we are brilliant and now everyone knows it! Yay us! Maybe they even give us the Phoenix bar assignment?*

FISH: *What did you just say?*

STAR: *Word on the street is there's a Phoenix bar floating around out there somewhere. Kind of came out of nowhere. You know, it's what they call the broken bits of Zeus's lightning bolt that are not supposed to exist.*

FISH: *I KNOW what a Phoenix bar is! What STREET?*

STAR: *I guess you weren't paying attention. Probably you were already daydreaming about Egypt.*

FISH: *This is big! We need to get in on this and we need to get in on it fast. Every hunter is going to be out for the Phoenix bar. It's the ultimate find. It makes Pegasus's necklace look like a pile of Legos.*

STAR: *So what do we do?*

FISH: *I have a plan.*

STAR: *Already?!*

FISH: *Yes.*

STAR: *Great. Here we go again.*

CHAPTER 44

PHOENIX

I WAKE UP THE MORNING AFTER FLYING HOME FROM Camp Timber Wolf to the sound of my father arguing with Great-Aunt Irma. Number one, it is loud. Number two, they *never* argue. Despite some aggressive jet lag, I drag my pajama-clad self out of bed and pad quietly down the stairs. They are in the kitchen, and the hallway provides perfect cover. If I stay low, they can't see me.

"Stop yelling, Lawrence," Great-Aunt Irma says. "You're going to wake up Lola."

"Are you kidding me?" he grumbles. "That kid could sleep through a hurricane." That's what you think. I edge a little closer. "I don't understand why you took the risk."

The last time I saw Dad, he was rescuing us from Liberty Island. He looked disheveled then, and he's moved on to being a downright mess. When Dad is focused on something particular, personal hygiene goes right out the window. His wild hair, standing up like he's been electrocuted, indicates he is onto something big.

"It was necessary," Great-Aunt Irma says curtly. "And it was my choice to help them."

"But the *danger*," Dad counters. "Like I told you, I think she's out there. I heard the necklaces, the sound they make. Nothing else makes that sound."

"I know, I know," Great-Aunt Irma says impatiently. "Crystal butterfly wings. The most delicate notes audible to the human ear. But you didn't *see* her. Your mind was probably playing tricks on you, which means you are freaking out over nothing. What do your sources say? You've contacted them, I assume?"

Dad's shoulders sag. "They know nothing," he says with a sigh. "But I'm convinced, Irma. Gryphon is out there."

I almost yelp. Gryphon? As in *Phoenix* and Gryphon?

"It doesn't matter," Great-Aunt Irma says dismissively. "I'm safe here. The Phoenix bars are safe here." Oh. *Dang.* This keeps getting better and better.

"Are you?" Dad shoots back. "How can you know that?"

"I have myself under very intense surveillance," she says with a sniff.

Dad throws up his hands. "Are you forgetting what Gryphon did?"

"The magic drove her crazy," Great-Aunt Irma says dismissively. "Could have happened to anyone."

"She tried to kill you." Dad turns toward the door, and I see the scowl etched on his face, a combination of anger, fear, and frustration.

"As if I could forget," Great-Aunt Irma replies.

"Gryphon wants the bars," Dad says quietly. "She wants the power. She's still searching—"

"You have no proof of that," Great-Aunt Irma interrupts.

"That does not mean it's not true!" Dad barks. "And now that you foolishly sent a bar to Lola using a *military* drone—don't even get me started on that—it's *out* there in circulation, floating around, untethered, up for grabs!"

Great-Aunt Irma narrows her gaze, focusing on Dad. I have never seen her look this way. Steely, determined, a little bit terrifying. Dad shrinks back. "Don't *ever* call me foolish," she says. "Lola and her team needed help, and I will always step in to help that child. She is special. She could be the best, better than you or me."

Dad moves his lips, but no sound comes out.

"And it would do you well to remember," Great-Aunt Irma continues, "that the only way to save the world and everyone in it was to hide the power of Zeus's lightning bolt. It was not my choice. It was my *duty*."

I suddenly feel dizzy. It's a good thing I'm low to the ground already because otherwise I might fall on my face. Great-Aunt Irma has the Phoenix bars, the broken parts of Zeus's lightning bolt, and she is the one who delivered it by drone so we could complete our mission. But that must mean . . . Can that *really* mean . . .

. . . that Great-Aunt Irma is the legendary *Phoenix*?

My great-aunt rests a reassuring hand on Dad's shoulder. "And don't forget," she says with a glint in her eye, "the phoenix *always* rises from the ashes."

No. *Way*.

ACKNOWLEDGMENTS

I WROTE THE BACK HALF AND MANAGED TWO revisions of *The Midnight Market* in quarantine. My office is in a building that shut down in March 2020, so I ended up at a card table in a tight corner of my bedroom. Out the large window, I watched the adorable out-of-control collie puppy and his overwhelmed owner; the redheaded jogger and the orange cat who followed along behind her, complaining; the exhausted mother with two young children on scooters; the guy with the ever-lengthening beard, yelling into his phone; the elderly couple, hand in hand; the neighbor across the street visiting with friends, spread many feet apart on her wide front deck.

My kids were down the hall, tucked in their rooms, faces bathed in blue light as they Zoomed through classes. No friends. No activities. Our cute downtown was empty, our streets were deserted, and an eerie silence hung over everything.

At first, I thought my heart would break. So much loss. So much pain. So much hopelessness.

But.

There were Lola Benko and friends, just waiting for me, on the page as they ever have been. I was so happy to be in their company, running around chasing magical objects and navigating a chaos that would never really hurt anyone. It was a relief.

It reminded me, as the months wore on and the staggering impact of the pandemic became clear, that it is only by looking away, even for a moment, that we can gather the resources to push through what we must. By indulging in escapism, be it a book, a movie, a TV show, a game of cards, a six-mile run just before the sun drops, a cake you've never baked before, whatever, we rebuild the strength to keep going. Not to quit. Not to give up.

I hope Lola provides an adventure for the mind, an escape from reality, a chance to recharge for young and old and everyone in between who needs it.

Happy reading, my friends.